Born to be Yours

Nidhi Kumar

Invincible Publishers

First published in India in 2019

ISBN : 978-93-88333-46-7

Invincible Publishers

Registered Address: 201A, SAS Tower, Sector 38,
Gurgaon-122003

Printed at Thomson Press (India) LTD

To my Mother, who always had faith in me and encouraged me to complete this book.

Acknowledgement

I would like to thank my parents who believed in me and always encouraged me to follow my dreams. With their support and love I was able to complete this book.

I would also like to thank my husband who stood by me through this journey of getting my book published.

Last but not the least, I would like to thank Mr. Ajay Setia, my editor Ms. Chandni Mathur and the entire team of Invincible Publication for converting my dream into reality.

Chapter 1

DELHI

"Who asked you to pick up my suitcase?"

I shouted aloud at the coolie amidst all the bustle created by people alighting from the train at the Delhi Railway Station. Other coolies were running after passengers in a frenzy, convincing them to let them carry their luggage. I had come to Delhi for the first time with dreams in my heart and a strong determination to achieve those dreams.

"What happened, Ananya?" asked my father, flabbergasted at the sight of me talking to the coolie in such a high pitch, which was a rare trait to be seen in me.

"Nothing, papa. He was picking up my luggage without my permission."

My father gave him a dirty look, demanding an explanation.

"I was just trying to help madam in carrying her luggage," said the coolie and retreated backwards into the crowd before my father could say anything. We were followed by a trail of coolies through the crowded station, pestering us to give our luggage to them and then pay them double just for having carried three suitcases from the platform to the taxi stand. However, my parents were ready to forgo their comfort and carried my big suitcases up the stairs themselves, dragging them brutally on. They had invested all their savings in my studies, which made even hiring a coolie for luggage a luxury we wouldn't afford.

I was born and brought up in a middle-class Punjabi family in Jaipur, under the guidance of my father Mr. Sudhanshu Malhotra who was working as a manager in a bank, and my mother Astha Malhotra who was a simple housewife. My father worked day and night just to ensure that he was able to give us all the comforts of life and a good education.

According to my mother, I was blessed with the potential to excel in my studies, complemented by my fair Punjabi complexion with a glowing dewy skin, sharp features, long glossy hair and a tall figure worthy of envy. However, some of my classmates were not quite impressed by my looks and considered me a nerdy bookworm, condemning me for having a boring life revolving around books.

Likewise, the boys were unmoved by my looks as I usually adorned myself with ill-fitted kurtas that put me out of their league of hot girls, but it did not matter to me as I was always busy studying.

My father hired a taxi outside the station after bargaining with the driver for ten minutes to reduce the price. Elated after his victory, he sat in the front seat along with the driver, while I chose to sit between Aryan, my younger brother, and my mother.

"Bhaiya, how much time will it take to reach the institute?" I asked, trying to control my losing pulse with the jerking motion of the car due to traffic at every red light.

"It depends on the traffic, madam," said the annoyed driver.

Aryan pinched me and said, "Di, are you in such a hurry to get rid of us?"

Slapping my little brother playfully, I held my mumma's hand as she was ready to explode with a running marathon of tears anytime.

"Mumma, don't worry. I will be alright," I said, wiping a small tear which was making its way out of the corner of her eye, having lied dormant there since we took the taxi I know beta she said squeezing my hand.

It was becoming more and more difficult for me now to hide my sprouting excitement and nervousness about reaching the college campus.

After paying the taxi driver, we entered the campus gate from where we were escorted by one of the guards to the reception for the submission of documents. This campus was quite big as compared to my previous college in Jaipur. A long cemented path lay before us, flanked by big vases along the path with flowers beautifully arranged in them. It was very unlike my previous college where the main building started just as one entered the main gate. On either side of this path, lush green landscaping had been done with a few benches under canopies of trees. It took us five minutes to reach the reception.

As we entered the reception, I was petrified to see the area jam-packed with students and their families running here and there for documentation. With a shining spotless floor and an artistically done false-ceiling that illuminated the entire place, the room seemed good enough to hold a small family function by Jaipur's standard. Two women were sitting across the reception desk and handling the paperwork with aplomb, as if they were born for it, without any trace of annoyance on their faces. Instead, a fake smile was plastered on both. Asking my parents to sit on a sofa which was luckily unoccupied, I made my way towards the reception.

One of the ladies looked up and said smilingly, "May I know your name, please?"

"Ananya." I responded

She picked up a form from her overly crowded desk and asked me to fill it up.

I had been selected by this college after I cracked the entrance test and then got grilled through the group discussion and interview rounds. Despite that, I felt thankful to such colleges that took pains going to small cities and gave the students there a platform to attain a higher degree, though the college also benefitted by enrolling good students from all over the country. The next step was to do background research about the college and its fee structure. It was out of my parents' budget, but they managed to get my admission done somehow by breaking all their fixed deposits. It was painful for me to see my parents sacrifice all that they had saved to support me in studying at a good college. I was also thankful to them for not forcing me to get married, as most parents would do at such a stage with their daughters.

I handed back the form at the reception where they placed the college seal on it.

After paying the fees, we decided to have a look at the college campus which was to the right of the reception, while the hostel was to the left. The classrooms were spacious with broad tables, a projector and revolving chairs as well. The rear end of the campus had a big auditorium which could contain more than 200 people. I guessed it was meant to conduct cultural programs and co-curricular activities.

After getting a glimpse of my college, we went to check out my hostel. It comprised of three buildings, painted red, surrounded by tall trees and a lush green garden.

We were escorted through the place by the hostel warden responsible for taking care of the girls. Her name was Tara and she looked strict with her deep set small eyes and a craggy complexion unsuccessfully hidden behind a mask of foundation.

"Ananya, only the rooms on third floor are left," said Tara, startling me with her shrill voice.

We all were breathing heavily by the time we reached the third floor and my mother was on the verge of collapsing any moment, but somehow she managed and Aryan cursed me all the way up as he was asked to drag my two suitcases to my room 'Ananya beta how will you manage to climb up and down so many stairs everyday?' Questioned my worried mother.

Before I could open my mouth, Tara answered quickly, "She will get used to it, don't worry."

. The third floor opened into a neat corridor with rooms on either side. Towards the end of the corridor, there was a water cooler kept for students. Tara opened the lock of a room and pushed open the door which creaked in protest. "The door needs some oiling," said Tara, sensing our reluctance to enter. "Ananya, come in and have a look at your room," said Tara grinning.

The room was well-maintained from inside. Two single beds were placed near the windows on one side of the room. Windows were framed in brown wood and were covered by peach curtains that matched the colour of the walls. Across the room from the beds, a long wooden table was fixed into the wall, meant to keep our belongings and to study. On the right side of the room, there were two small cupboards. My parents inspected through everything like CBI officers.

"Ananya, did you like the room?" asked my overjoyed father. He simply wanted to buy every possible happiness for his daughter, even though he lacked the resources.

"Yes, papa. It's good." I was acutely aware of how tough it was for my father to manage after all that he had spent on my studies.

Having observing my new space with critical eyes and obsessively worrying over how will I manage with the basics, soon it was time for them to leave. We parted with teary eyes and they blessed me to face the givings of life all alone. As I was about to sit, there was a knock on the door. I dragged myself to open the door and was startled to see Tara again.

"Ananya, look who's there," said Tara in her shrill voice. But the very next moment, she pushed me aside and opened the door herself. I then got my first glimpse of the person standing behind her.

She was beautiful, my height, and with big baby-doll eyes fringed by long lashes. Her velvety skin shone like a diamond, as if she had come directly from a salon. She was wearing a beautiful off-white off-shoulder top and tight-fitting black pants along with high heels.

"Hi, I'm Niya," she said, bringing her hand forward and blinking twice.

"I'm Ananya. Nice to meet you, Niya. Please come in."

She came in with two big suitcases, one red and one yellow. She seemed to me a rich spoilt kid who was used to splurging her parents' money. Niya took a quick glance around the room and the annoyed look on her face told me that she did not like it.

"Do you have another room, warden?" asked Niya in her sweet voice.

"Sweetie, this is all that I can offer you," said Tara in an expressionless manner.

A long hiss escaped Niya's mouth as she slouched down on her bed disappointed. One's perception can instantly change the value of a place. Till five minutes ago, I was thinking myself lucky to have got this room, but now, I couldn't help but think that there was something wrong with it. Tara looked at both of us and said, "Enjoy your stay, girls." The next second, she was out the door and it shut with a loud thud.

"Okay, let me introduce myself properly," Niya said, making a small pout. "I'm from Bangalore and have come here to study just because I got bored of answering my interfering parents who don't have time for me. What about you?"

I was shocked to hear her words. She was far too upright and the complete opposite of me with regard to our respective parents. Mine meant the world to me. She looked at me wide-eyed. "Hey, what happened, Ananya? Did I say something wrong? Anyway, this is how I am. You will get used to it," she said and winked. "So, what about you?" she asked as she started unpacking her suitcase.

"Have you come here alone?" was my first question.

"Oh, yes," she smiled again, "My parents were busy, so I came on my own. I studied at a boarding school all my childhood so I am used to it, no worries."

"So, where are you from?" she asked smiling.

"I'm from Jaipur."

"Oh, the pink city," she exclaimed and started unpacking her things. She stopped for a second and said, "Ananya, which bed would you like to take?"

"The one next to the window," I quipped without giving her any time to take her decision first.

Over the next hour, both of us unpacked and arranged our things without talking much. Niya broke the silence then by saying, "Hey Ananya, do you want to eat something? I'm starving."

"Yes, even I'm feeling very hungry, but our mess has not opened yet. It will take them another two hours to open."

"What!?" shrieked Niya like a small baby who is denied instant gratification. "I'm dying of hunger. I can't wait for this mess to open. Let's go out and eat something."

"But Niya, we are new to this place and I don't even know where to go."

"Ananya, if we think like this, we will always be new to this place, darling. We need to explore new places in order to know it. Don't waste time now, let's go unless you want to sit here and starve."

For a moment, I thought she was being manipulative, but then I was starving too, so I decided to go out with her. Reaching downstairs Niya asked the gatekeeper uncle regarding any market nearby. He, in turn, flashed all his yellow teeth at us and blushed, looking at Niya.

"Ma'am, there is one just across the road. Go straight through that narrow lane and you'll find a big market and some good restaurants there."

Niya gave me a broad smile and said, "See, Ananya, I told you we only need to explore in order to gain knowledge."

"Yeah, and we need to look good as well," I said, making Niya blush. While walking in the direction we were given, I spotted a small dhaba in some distance and thought of suggesting it to Niya, but hesitated the next moment, wondering if a rich girl like her would eat at such a place. To my surprise, however, Niya said, "Here we are!" as we reached the dhaba. "It looks clean and hygienic. Let's eat here."

Seeing my bewildered expression, she said, "Girl, don't be shocked. One can get very tasty food at such dhabas. Better than they serve at a restaurant even," and pulled me inside.

The food was delicious indeed. We were so famished that we gobbled everything down that was served to us. The talking didn't happen much. Mostly we stuck to how tasty the food was and what each of us preferred over the other. We came back tired after exploring the market and started preparing for the next day—our first day at college

Chapter 2

I woke up at 7 in the morning and was not surprised to see Niya still in bed. I quickly went to the washroom so that I may get ready before she woke up as there was only one washroom.

'Good morning, Ananya.' Said Niya when she saw me coming out of the washroom.

'Good morning, Niya. Get ready soon or we will be late on our first day.'

Niya got ready in fifteen minutes wearing a pink top and black trouser making me feel out of place, as I was wearing a long kurta and jeans. She looked at me from head to toe and I was ready to be attacked again about my clothes, but she smiled and complimented, 'You are a beauty in disguise Ananya.'

'Thanks Niya', I liked the fact that she did not judge me from my clothes. Rather she complimented me for my beauty. It felt like a big deal coming from her. I don't know why.

As we reached our college we could see everybody hovering around the boards . I went close to the boards to have a glimpse of what was written on them but soon I lost the battle and started feeling suffocated amidst the swelling crowd so I moved out from there to find Niya and saw her standing and smiling with a tall and handsome guy. Her attention got drifted from the hunk when she saw me approaching and said, ' Don't worry Ananya, it's just our sections displayed on the board. Meet him…' said Niya pointing at the boy standing next to her. 'He is Karan.'

I said a curt hello to him and faced the other side. Karan looked at Niya and said, 'Chalo, lets meet after class.' Making Niya give him her attractive smile in return.

In 10 minutes we both were sitting in a our seperate classrooms.

The first day of class–a new beginning and new dreams to pursue–brought with it a certain nervousness. Everybody was well-dressed according to the latest fashion, making me wonder how out of place I looked. I had never had the chance since my adolescence to develop a fashion sense as the only thing on my mind had been studying hard. Out of habit, I chose to sit on the first bench. The boy to whom Niya was talking few minutes before entered the class just then. He saw me and smiled, then took a seat on the second bench. The class was fully packed now with boys and girls who were busy chatting with their partners in hushed voices. A bell rang and everybody got attentive. In a minute, a tall woman who seemed to be in her early thirties entered the class. She had a wheatish complexion and was clad in a purple silk to saree

'Good morning class.' She said in her south Indian accent. 'My name is Sridevi Iyer and I will be teaching you Economics. Welcome, all of you.'

'Thank you Mam,' everybody shouted in unison and with a lot of excitement for the first day.

'She is going to torture us with her accent and economics', said a guy sitting behind with Karan.

'Today we will have an interactive session to know each other. So tell me your names and the place you come from.' She pointed towards me and said, 'Yes young lady, we will start with you.'

I stood up nervously and said in a fumbling voice, 'I'm Ananya from Jaipur.' Gradually it was the turn of the entire class and everybody gave their introductions. Our first class was over and was a real fun followed by two more classes and then came the lunch time. Everybody was eager to go to the cafeteria to have lunch and to get to know their new friends better. The cafeteria was big enough for about 100 students, but still, it seemed overcrowded. I quickly grabbed a seat in the corner alone, finished my lunch and went back to attend the last class of the day. I came back tired and collapsed in my bed waiting for Niya who still had a class left. While laying down there in the softness of my freshly thwarted mattress I was thinking how mumma used to come running after me with my clothes when I was back from college and then how the delicious lunch waited for me every afternoon, how I would laze around while mumma ran errands for me. Times have changed. Now I will have to do my own running. I was contemplating how I would manage this new era of my life when I was brought back to the reality by a phone call. I picked up the phone with a cheerful smile spread across my face. 'Hi, mumma!'

'How are you, beta? We all are missing you so much.'

'Me too, mom', I whispered with tears flashing around the corners of my eyes

'How was your first day in college beta?' Came her soothing voice from the other end.

'It was good, mumma. I made so many new friends.' I chirped proudly.

My mother's tone suddenly changed from polite to a little brash in a nanosecond. How women master this art of switching themselves in so many characters at once is truly amazing. 'Ananya, remember to stay away from bad company and make friends with good girls.' The last word was given undue pressure. Girls. I knew she exactly meant—stay away from boys. My mother was uncharacterstically worried with me falling for a wicked guy so she had sworn me over that I would stay away from boys, in general.

'Ok, mom.' I said feigning boredom. 'I will call you later. Somebody is knocking at the door,' I said as I opened the door. From the other side of the door came, 'I am so tired,' and having said that Niya entered the room and collapsed animatedly on her bed, making me laugh.

Chapter 3

I made up my mind to not restrict myself from mingling with my classmates. In order to know them, I had to talk to them. So, instead of sitting on the first bench, I went and sat on the fourth, where I saw a beautiful girl sitting beside Karan.

"Hey, you are Ananya, right?" asked the girl.

"Yes, and you must be Bhavika," I replied.

"Yeah, and he is Karan," said Bhavika, smiling.

Karan smiled and said, "We both know each other. We met yesterday and Ananya did not talk to me properly." My face turned red with embarrassment as I remembered how rude I had been to him.

"Hey, that's okay," said Karan upon seeing my face. "I can understand, as we all are new to the place, but we should not judge people on our first meeting. Anyway, it was nice meeting you, Ananya."

"Same here, Karan," I replied meekly.

Karan was tall with a good build. His clear complexion and a warm smile had the ability to melt any girl's heart. We quickly stepped up to talking like old friends, exchanging information about each other till our class started.

During lunch time, the three of us went to sit in the cafeteria. Somebody patted on my back and, to my happy surprise, it was Niya who had come to tell me that she was going back to the hostel as she had no other class for the day. Before leaving, she said, "Hi Karan, how are you?" making him blush.

Seeing this, Bhavika started giggling and said, "Karan, why don't you tell Niya that you like her?"

"What? I can't believe one of my friends has a crush on my roommate!" I exclaimed.

"Ananya, please don't tell Niya. It's too early."

"Okay, Karan," I grinned back, "But tell her soon."

After lunch, Mr. Rustogi — our Environmental Studies teacher entered the class with two boys at his heels and said, "These two are your new classmates." He then turned to them and said, "Introduce yourself," wiping his spectacles.

"Hi, I'm Varun. I am from Bihar," said one.

"I'm Sahil, from Bangalore," said the other, without any trace of a smile on his face. He was really good-looking, tall with a toned body. He had a wheatish skin tone, intense eyes with thick eyebrows and curly hair. He had been bestowed with a sharp straight nose and soft lips which were drawn a little forward like a barely visible pout, complimenting his dimpled chin. The only thing missing from his face was a smile, which made him seem as if he was upset about something.

"Oh, he seems to be grumpy," said Bhavika. "Why does God make all good-looking people like this?"

He sat alone for all four lectures that day, listening attentively and jotting down notes for each, and was the first one to move out of class too.

We had started getting assignments by then, which gave us very little time to engage in our new friendships over the weekend. Niya and I were both busy completing our Economics assignment when I got a call from Karan and he asked me to come downstairs along with Niya. Niya smiled and said, "Well well, seems like your friends cannot live without you."

"It was Karan. He has asked both of us to come downstairs," I said. I could sense her body stiffen at the mention of Karan, but she somehow managed to give me her beautiful smile and said, "No yaar, what will I do between you two?"

"Niya, he wants to meet you especially."

She jumped from her bed and said, "Really? But why?"

"Because I think that Karan likes you."

Niya blushed and said, "Ananya, you are not joking with me, right?"

"Niya, you have mutual feeling towards him too. Why do you not tell him?"

"Anu, I thought it was too early to tell him. Secondly, I thought you like Karan. That's why I withdrew myself from him."

I was shocked at her words for a second and asked, "Niya, what made you think like this?"

"Anu, I saw you talking to him many times in college, so I thought maybe you guys were interested in each other."

"Bullshit, Niya. He is a good friend of mine, and half the time he is talking about you."

"Ananya, let's not waste our time anymore and get ready before another girl steals my Karan from me. I would have sacrificed him for you easily, but not for any other girl," she said and we started giggling.

Karan was patiently waiting for us downstairs and a smile crept onto his face upon seeing Niya. "Hi girls, you took your sweet time to show up," he said.

"Sorry," said Niya. "I was not able to decide on what to wear."

"You look pretty in whatever you wear, Niya," said Karan. Both continued to look at each other cluelessly. I cleared my throat and said, "Let's go and sit somewhere."

We went to McD, ordered a burger and french fries, and chatted for a long time. Niya and Karan were stealing glances at each other, so I decided to leave them alone for some time and walked out to talk to my mom on call. Karan and Niya followed out after ten minutes and he gave her a big bear hug.

"So...what happened, Niya?" I teased her as we reached our hostel and she blushed like a seventeen year old girl.

"He proposed to me, Ananya."

"Really? What did you say?"

I accepted his proposal. I really think he is the kind of guy who can handle my free-spiritedness, being so calm and patient himself."

I smiled and said, "God bless you both."

"Anu, stop acting like an old aunt."

The next day, Mrs. Iyer entered the classroom, followed by Sahil. He was wearing a crisp white shirt with blue denims and had a little beard on his face which made him charmingly attractive. Even I had trouble shifting my gaze away from him. He had something which really attracted me towards him. He looked at nobody and went to sit with Ronan, the most mischievous boy of our class, at the last bench.

"You are going to have a quick surprise test now," said Mrs. Iyer, taking our breath away. Students started to panic, causing a stir in the classroom. Mrs. Iyer shouted at the top of her voice, "Silence! Don't behave like school-going students and sit on either side of the bench, leaving the middle seat vacant. Ananya, stand up and go sit at the last bench with Sahil. Ronan, you come and sit in the front."

I turned around and saw Sahil looking at me. Only the next moment, he bowed his head down, ignoring me. My heart started palpitating vigorously, making me go completely out of breath as I slowly made my way towards him. Waves of nervousness went tingling down to my fingertips. I don't know what was happening to me. I had only been asked to sit next to him. Sahil made no effort to say hi as I approached the last desk and looked the other way.

"Hi, I'm Ananya," I said after gathering some courage. He looked towards me for a second and said, "Hi, you already know my name."

"Arrogant monster," I mumbled. Sahil was the first one to turn in his completed test, naturally putting himself in the category of intelligent students. I never saw him during lunch time, or even talking to anybody or mixing up with other students. He always stayed aloof, as if something was continuously on his mind. I couldn't help but think about him. I tried to change my mood, but I wanted to look at him once more before going back to the hostel. Niya was with me as she did not have any other class either.

"Anu, what happened? Are you okay?" asked Niya.

"Yes, Niya. I'm fine." I got lucky and saw him standing under a tree, talking on the phone.

This time, however, there was no gloom on his face. Instead, he was smiling. Then I saw those cute little dimples on his face, which made him look even more attractive.

So, Mr. Rude knows how to smile as well. My heart started pounding faster, but out of jealousy this time. I wondered whom he might be speaking to on call, perhaps his girlfriend. I felt myself in a pool of remorse with a heart-ache quite unknown to me. Niya shook me out of my reverie and said, "Anu what's wrong? Who is that guy you are staring at?"

I collected myself and said, "He is in my class and is very arrogant."

That's the reason you are staring at him said Niya making me blush. He saw me looking at him and caught my eye for a second, then faced the other way with the same old gloomy expression, making me feel as if somebody has pierced my heart with a knife.

I was not able to sleep that night; his smile lingered in my thoughts, making it difficult for me to erase his face from my mind. Whenever I closed my eyes, I saw his face with his beautiful dimples.

"Anu, what happened? Are you missing your family?" asked Niya as she was also awake and talking to Karan. She might have seen me tossing and turning in bed.

"No, Niya. I'm just not able to sleep."

I hope I'm not disturbing you because of my phone."

"Oh no, Niya. Carry on your sweet talk, I'm enjoying it."

She smiled at me coyly and threw a pillow at me. I turned to the other side and started pondering over the fact that I might do the same if I ever fell in love – talking on the phone late at night, waiting for his phone call, and saying 'I love you' at the smallest of things. This brought Sahil back to my thoughts, making me fantasise what it would be like if Sahil and I ever got together. His apparent disinterest and perhaps the existence of a girlfriend kept these thoughts in check and I fell asleep thinking about him.

Chapter 4

"Anu, why are you taking so long to get ready today?" shouted Niya. "You are behaving exactly like me. Are you okay?"

"Niya, I don't know what to wear today. It seems as if I have nothing to wear," I responded.

This brought a smirk on Niya's face. "Hey, what's going on? You are behaving in a very strange manner."

"Niya, I think I need to do some shopping. These clothes of mine are quite out of fashion."

"Yeah, sure. We can go to Lajpath Nagar to do some shopping this weekend. It's the hub of all latest fashion. As for today, don't worry. You can take anything from my closet."

"Are you sure, Niya?"

"Oh yes, my baby. You need not be formal with me."

I picked out a white body-hugging top that had purple dots all over. It beautifully enhanced my curves that were otherwise always hidden under my ill-fitted long kurtas. I left my hair loose over my shoulders. Love had started changing me and I was not even aware of it. Niya looked at me with a dropped jaw. "Anu, you are so beautiful. I don't know what makes you dress up like a behenji."

"I don't know, Niya. I am just more comfortable wearing my kurta and jeans."

Forget about your ill-fitted kurtas and jeans. I will help you do the shopping this time. You are staying in a metro city now, and you should dress like a metro girl."

I felt a bit apprehensive entering the class that day as everybody was staring at me. I even caught Ronan gawking at me.

Bhavika screamed upon seeing me, "Anu, wow! You look so beautiful."

Karan seemed like he was searching for words. "Anu, you are looking fab today," he said finally, regaining his composure.

"Thanks, Karan and Bhavika."

My heart was pounding now as my gaze rested at the door. Finally, Mrs. Iyer and Sahil entered the classroom together.

"Class, here are your test papers and I must say, you all did horribly except a few. Sahil and Ananya secured full marks," said Mrs. Iyer, making everybody clap for us. I noticed Sahil staring at me for the first time, but I was unable to make out whether he was looking at me with resentment or appreciation.

"What kind of a boy is Sahil? Doesn't he talk to anybody?" asked Bhavika during lunch. "But he is also so cute. I would really like to talk to him," she said, fluttering her eyelashes. "There is something about him which attracts me."

My facial muscles tightened. It was as if she had snatched the words right out of my mouth ruthlessly.

"Ananya, are you alright?" asked Karan, looking at my tensed face.

"Yeah, Karan. I'm okay."

We returned to our class and I saw Sahil standing in the corridor, looking out of the window. "Shall I go and talk to him? There is still time for the class to start," said the excited Bhavika.

"Bhavika, why are you in such a hurry? He looks quite disinterested anyway," said Karan.

"So what, yaar? Let me try at least. He is making me go crazy and I don't want any other stupid girl to propose to him before I do."

I felt as if somebody had stabbed me in my heart, but still I smiled so that Karan wouldn't notice and say anything to Niya. Bhavika was a good friend, but I still wished that Sahil did not reciprocate her feelings. Bhavika was a pretty girl and I was worried that perhaps Sahil would fall for her too.

Zillions of thoughts were rushing through my mind, making me sweat a little. Bhavika started to walk towards him slowly, as if second guessing her own decision.

"Hi Sahil, how are you?" she initiated.

"I'm fine," said Mr. Arrogant and turned to look the other way.

"Can you please help me out with my next assignment?" she asked.

He was now standing face to face with her. He looked at her and then glanced at me, holding my gaze for a second. Returning his gaze to her, he said in his deep arrogant voice, "You already have an intelligent girl in your group. Why don't you ask her for help?" and then went straight into the class, leaving Bhavika standing like a fool.

Bhavika strode on angrily towards us and said, "He is so rude. How dare he?"

"Calm down, Bhavika," said Karan. "I warned you beforehand. Anyway, don't worry. You are just too beautiful for him. We will find some decent guy for you."

I couldn't help but think that if he had behaved this way with Bhavika, how would he treat me. "Oh God, please don't put feeling in my heart for this stone-hearted rude person."

It was Mr. Rustogi's class next. Wiping his dirty spectacles with a dirty tissue paper, he said, "Today we will play a game to see how much you all know about each other." Everyone's face lit up with excitement.

The class was divided into two groups. One group was asked to make chits with their names on it, while the other group took these chits, one each, to reveal their respective partners. Each partner was supposed to say what they knew about the other. To my luck, good or bad, I got Sahil's name in mine. Bhavika stuck her thumb up and said, "All the best."

This funny game was quite a relaxing activity for our usual hectic schedule. Many students said very funny things about each other. Finally, it was Sahil's turn. I was petrified by the thought of him talking about me.

"I don't know anything about this girl," he said, looking towards me.

His words *'this girl'* infuriated me. I said, "Excuse me, my name is Ananya."

Mr Rastogi interrupted us, sensing that the situation was getting out of hand. "Sahil, it's been more than a month now. Say anything, whatever you know," he said.

"Okay, one of her friends is so irritating, she asked me for my help to complete her assignment." His words created a major stir in the classroom as everybody knew that he was talking about Bhavika. Bhavika herself was on the verge of crying. Mr. Rustogi simply asked Sahil to be seated. It was my turn now.

I started, "He is the most arrogant person I have ever come across." Sahil stared at me and smiled for the first time in class. His cute dimpled smile made me go weak for a second, but then I turned my gaze away from him. "This boy knows nothing about friendship," I continued. "My friend had just asked him for help, and he insulted her. I don't know what he thinks of himself."

Sahil placed a hand on his head and arched his eyebrow to stare at me. The rest of the class was enjoying and agreeing with me. Tanya shouted, "Sahil, why are you so rude to her? Can't you see, she is dying to talk to you?"

This brought another smile to Sahil's face. I stood dumbstruck, searching for words and sweating profusely. 'How did Tanya come to know about my feeling for Sahil?' I wondered. Perhaps she had noticed me looking at him.

Karan saw me go pale, so he interrupted and said, "Tanya, why are you saying all this bullshit?"

"Karan, she is your friend and you don't know how she feels about Sahil ," said Tanya in a mocking way.

I gathered some strength and said, "What rubbish, Tanya? Just remain in your limits."

"Stop this nonsense and carry on your love life outside the class. I started this game so that you all could know each other better. The class is over," thundered Mr. Rastogi and walked out of the classroom angrily. I scrambled back to my seat without looking at Sahil. Sahil frowned and walked out of the classroom as if somebody had insulted him.

Karan was studying me carefully. "Anu, don't worry. Everyone will forget everything soon. You just relax," he said to calm me down.

During lunch that day, Niya came and hugged me tightly. I knew by her hug that Karan had already informed her about the incident. Something came over me and I cried for the first time while hugging her.

Niya wiped my face and asked me, "Is it the same guy who was talking on the phone that day?"

I could only nod in response.

"What is going on, Anu?" she asked in a concerned tone. "I asked you the same question a few days ago and you just bluffed me. If you consider me your friend, please tell me what's in your heart and we will try to figure it out, Anu. Don't keep everything to yourself and suffer silently. We both are friends, right?"

"I don't know, Niya, what is happening with me. I am not able to sleep and I am followed by him all the time in my dreams. I know he is rude, but my eyes still yearn to have just one glimpse of him. I'm awestruck by his smile. I tried to hate him, but I'm not able to do that."

Niya smiled this time, but with compassion. "Oh, Anu. You are in love."

I didn't want to hear it, but it was the truth. I was in love with Mr. Arrogant. "What do I do now, Niya?"

"Just enjoy these moments, Anu, and go with the flow. I cannot tell you to be happy because that guy is a complete stranger to us. Just beware of him as he knows how you feel about him now," said Niya and hugged me again.

Chapter 5

The next morning, I did not feel like going to college. I felt as if something heavy was placed over my heart, suffocating me to death. Niya was almost ready when she said, "Anu, get up. We are late."

"Niya, I don't feel like going to college today."

Niya came and sat beside me on my bed and said, "Anu, I know you are saying this because of what happened yesterday, but you can't be weak like this. You have done nothing to be so embarrassed about. If you don't go to college today, everybody is going to think that what Tanya said was right. Just go and pretend as if nothing happened. Karan is there to support you anyway."

"Niya, you told Karan?"

"Yes, I did so that he may take care of you. You know, Anu, he really cares for you like I do."

"Yes, I know, Niya. He cares a lot for me, but less than you do."

Niya pinched my cheek and said, "Get ready, my baby in love."

I reached college on time and found Karan waiting for me at the gate. "Don't worry, Anu. Let's go to class," he said.

I found Sahil standing in the corridor. When he saw me, he turned the other side. It made my heart ache even more. I complained to God for having given me such beautiful emotions for this arrogant fellow. Everybody in class stared at me initially, but when they saw I was not affected by it, things returned to normalcy. When I was about to sit, Bhavika stood up to move to another table. I held her hand and asked, "What is the matter? Why are you not sitting here?"

She jerked her hand away and said, "You are not my friend. You know, Ananya, that I liked Sahil, yet you started liking him."

Karan intervened and said, "What is wrong with you, Bhavika? She was fighting for you in front of the whole class yesterday."

"Oh, stop it, Karan. I know why you are taking her side. It is because of your girlfriend," she said and moved away to sit with Ronan who was more than happy to sit with her.

I was about to stop Bhavika, but Karan held my hand and said, "Ananya, let her go. She doesn't deserve our friendship."and this announced the end of our friendship

Despite the back-breaking syllabus and the huge number of assignments, my day did not feel complete till I looked at Sahil, even though he seemed disinterested in me. Days passed by too quickly along with his presence.

Chapter 6

Mrs. Iyer entered the class with a smile on her face and said, "Here is your date sheet for your first semester exams that will start after a month." Her words created chaos in the class, making Mrs. Iyer slam the duster down on the table. "Silence!" she screamed.stop behaving like school going kids and start preparing for your exams.

The last 20 days were quite monotonous and everybody was busy making notes and studying hard.. As the exam date drew closer the number of absentees increased especially those who have started studying late.

Sahil came everyday to the class with his same brooding trademark but the only thing which changed was he used to look at me once in a day.

We buried ourselves in our books day and night forgetting about everything else and for a change even I stop thinking about Sahil as my mind got occupied with books. Finally with a month of self inflicted torture to study hard our exams got over and Niya and I just collapsed on our beds coming back from our college as we were sleep deprived. We just woke up to have our dinner and then we agin slept as if we were facing a jet lag suitation

The next morning was beautiful as I woke up dreaming about him. Niya was still asleep, perhaps dreaming about Karan. Love is the strongest of all emotions and requires a lot of nurturing in order to blossom, and here I had fallen in love with the strangest person about whom I knew nothing. I felt drawn toward him like a moth to a flame; his mere presence in class gave me butterflies in the stomach. I needed to do something about it, lest it lead to an emotional breakdown, so I decided to talk to him.

We were supposed to submit our last assignment of that session that day. When Karan and I reached the class, Mr. Arrogant was already sitting there, making last minute checks on his assignment. I wondered how many times he must have checked it. As nobody else was in the class besides us at the moment, I decided to talk to him. He got alarmed upon seeing me walking towards him.

"Sahil," I stammered reaching close to his seat but before I could say anything, his phone rang and he gestured with his hand for me to stop . All his tension evaporated like dew in the afternoon and that charming smile of his was back as he stood up and walked away to a corner to speak, leaving me standing like a fool. I burned with jealousy and anger. Unable to bear this insult anymore, I made my way towards Sahil. Karan yelled at me from behind to stop me, but it was in vain as I tightly held Sahil's hand, pulled him around to make him face me and snatched his phone. He looked at me shocked and taken by complete surprise.

I held his phone to my ear and heard a soft sweet voice that said, "Chachu, I miss you so much. Please come home soon." I felt hesitant to hand the phone back to Sahil and looked at him meekly like a lamb trapped in a cage due to its own folly. This time, Sahil came close to me, held my hand tightly and pulled me out of the classroom as the class had started getting filled with other students. I was frightened to death, but loved the way he held my hand and was taking me away with him to talk. He could have insulted me in front of our other classmates and I wouldn't even have minded it, but he didn't. Sahil led me outside our class and into a stranded corridor before leaving my hand. It had turned red under his angry grip. Glaring me down, he uttered my name for the first time as he started, "Yes, Miss Ananya, who gave you the right to snatch my phone from me and who do you think I was talking to? My girlfriend? And even if I was, you have no right to interfere in my life. I know you have been trying to do it for a long time."

I could say nothing but just look at him. All my anger and ego has flown out of the window. Sahil remained quiet for a second and looked amused at the way I was looking at him. It might have calmed him down a little because the next thing he said was, "Ananya, I'm talking to you," giving me a little shake.

"Do you have a girlfriend?" I asked. Anger sprouted in his eyes, turning them red.

"Why don't you mind your own business, Ananya?" he said, crossing his arms across his chest, showing disinterest.

"I asked you something, Sahil. Do you have a girlfriend?" I asked again, raising my voice a little this time. I don't know where I was drawing so much courage from.

"No!" he shouted in a frustrated manner. "I don't have a girlfriend. I have not come here to make girlfriends and party."

It was becoming more and more difficult for me to hide my feelings from him now, particularly when he was standing so close to me and had held my hand for the first time too.

I leaned in to him and touched my lips to his. He froze in his spot while I ran back to the class. Mrs. Iyer had collected all the assignments by then. When she saw me at the gate, Sahil following close behind, she angrily said, "Please don't come late into my classes for stupid reasons."

Karan gave me a worried look and asked, "All well?" I just smiled at him in response. Sahil kept stealing glances at me throughout that class.

During lunchtime, I was kidnapped by my two best friends to a secluded place in our college as they wanted to know everything. "Anu, please stop killing me with this suspense. Tell me what happened!" Niya asked.

Taking a deep breath, I said, "Sahil doesn't have a girlfriend."

Niya shrieked and jumped with happiness. Karan kept his hand over her mouth and said, "Calm down, Niya."

"...and I kissed him," I said sheepishly.

Niya's jaw fell open and I extended my hand to shut it. "Anu, I thought I was the most daring amongst us all, but you proved me wrong."

Karan started laughing and said, "Aww, poor Sahil. He seemed so shaken up. Anu, did he say something to you in return?"

"No, I ran back to the class before he could say anything."

I came back to class after giving every deatail about my encounter with Sahil.

The only thing that had changed in his attitude since the incident was that he had started glancing at me, but he was an awesome pretender at that too.

We were waiting for Mrs Iyer and When Karan saw Sahil entering the class, he gestured at him to sit with us. I was sure that he would refuse, but to my surprise, Mr. Arrogant came and sat between me and Karan.

Nervousness started to engulf me from within, but I remained calm outside. With falling in love, I had also learnt the art of deception, of hiding my inner feelings and not letting them show on my face. We both looked at each other for a minute, after which he shifted his gaze to look the other way. There had been no nervousness the previous day when I had snatched his phone away, but today I was drowning in this feeling. Mrs. Iyer saw Sahil sitting next to me and was annoyed by it. Sahil also notice her reaction, then turned to look at me. I raised my eyebrow and said, "What? Don't blame me, Sahil, if Mrs. Iyer is so possessive about you. I hope you are not in love with her..."

"What?" said Sahil, laughing for the first time.

Karan was astonished to see Sahil laughing, and asked me, "Anu, what joke are you cracking? Involve me as well."

Sahil looked at me in a cute manner and said, "Ananya, you are such a baby."

"Mr. Sahil, I'm not a baby, mind it." Our results were announced that day and nobody was shocked to find out that Sahil had topped the class, followed by me. Karan had managed to get a good score too.

"Nobody can beat me," said Sahil, glancing at me. I was sure now that he was enjoying putting me down.

I stood up in frustration and mumbled, "Better luck next time." I pushed my chair back and walked past Karan and Sahil, my legs brushing against theirs, as there was no space.

Sahil called after me, saying, "Can't you say 'excuse me'?" Before I could say anything in response, he said laughingly, "It's okay, you are a small baby. No need to apologize," making Karan laugh too.

I stomped my feet on the floor and said, "Karan, I will see you later." I stormed out of the classroom and ran into Niya at the cafe. I was so engrossed in my thoughts that she had to clap in front of my face to draw me out of them. "Congrats, Anu. Stop thinking about Sahil all the time," she said.

"Thank you, Niya. I was not thinking about that monster," I said.

She giggled and said, "Liar! And before you asked me, Anu, I passed with flying colours."

Karan arrived just then and told Niya how Sahil and I had sat together in class that day. I stared at Karan and he suppressed a smile. He held my hand and said, "Anu, you both looked so cute teasing each other, and I couldn't believe my eyes that the boy who was not interested in talking to anybody was teasing you, Anu. I have a feeling that Sahil has some feeling for you too, that's why he agreed to sit with you."

The next few days at college were quite busy as studies for the second semester had begun in full swing, keeping us occupied with new assignment and presentations. Sahil started to sit with us regularly now. Once, his phone rang while he was sitting next to me but he did not move aside to take his call.

He told me himself later that his brother's daughter Reem was very close to him and called him everyday.

"How old is Reem?" I asked.

"She will turn four tomorrow. We actually share our birthdays," he replied and immediately bit his tongue.

"Wow, it's your birthday tomorrow!" I exclaimed.

He turned gloomy now and said, "I know, but I don't celebrate my birthday. It's just a waste of time."

"How is that possible? You must not have good friends like us, that's why you never celebrated your birthday."

"This is the reason, Anu, that I stay away from friendship. I don't like my friends pestering me for small things."

"This is what friendship is all about, Sahil – enjoying every moment with your friends and forgetting your worries."

He nodded in a gesture of giving up, but glanced at me wordlessly with love.

Sahil broke his gaze away from me and said, "She is not my girlfriend."

I felt as if a big heavy thing had fallen on my heart, rendering me unable to breathe. Niya could sense my agony as I was about to cry, so she held my hand and said, "Anu, let's go. This boy only knows how to hurt you and is not meant for you." She turned around and said to Sahil, "I will make sure that she does not annoy you anymore. And Karan, if you continue talking to this insensitive rude fellow, I will not continue my relationship with you either."

Karan looked at Sahil and said, "What is wrong with you, man?" and left with us.

I cried like a baby all the way back to the hostel. It felt like my world had come to an end, that his love was the only life line for me to exist, but it had snapped now.

"Anu, please stop crying. That boy is a rude monkey. He will never understand your love. Don't waste your time on some dumbass who doesn't even know how to respect you,"

After crying for hours, I fell asleep. It was around 2 AM when my phone beeped, but I felt too tired to push open my eyelids heavy with the weight of tears just shed.

When I finally did, I saw that it was a message from Sahil. It said, 'I'm sorry, Anu. My intention was not to hurt you, but if somebody comes and acknowledges you as my girlfriend, which is not true, it will definitely make me lose my temper. I hope you understand.'

Without replying, I turned the phone away and went back to sleep.

Chapter 8

I woke up late the next morning and saw Niya sitting beside me. She had got breakfast packed for me in her lunch–box as she had not wanted to disturb me. I had a severe headache because of all the crying and oversleeping, but I felt better after having my breakfast. Niya got a call from Karan who asked her to come down and she dragged me along as well. I reached downstairs only to find Sahil sitting with Karan, and I took a U–turn. Niya stopped me and pulled me back, saying, "Anu, please." Unable to control my emotions anymore, I started crying. My first rejection had become too much for me to handle.

Before I could leave, Sahil stood up, walked over to me and said, "Stop crying like this, Ananya. You look so drained already. I'm sorry. How many times would you like me to say sorry now?"

"I don't want your sorry, just get lost," I said and turned to leave, but he did not let me go. This time, he pulled me back and held me tightly by my waist to turn me towards him. He brought me closer to himself, kissed me on both my cheeks and said, "Baby, I'm sorry. Please forgive your boyfriend." His words came as a shock to me. I stood there like a statue being hugged by the man I had loved for the first time in life, but my hands remained numb and motionless. He whispered in my ear, "Ananya, I love you. Do you hear me?"

It was unbelievable for me that the boy who had said just the previous night that I was not his girlfriend was now saying that he loved me. How could someone be so unpredictable!He was now looking directly into my eyes, not apprehensive regarding anybody around him. "Anu, will you say something or just keep standing like a statue?" I blinked twice and asked, "What did you say just now?"

His lips curled up in a smirk as he pulled my cheek and said, "You want to hear it again?" A few of our batchmates around us were staring at us wide-eyed. Oddly conscious of the fact, Karan and Niya suggested that we went elsewhere and dragged us outside. Sahil and I couldn't take our eyes off of each other. We went to a café nearby. Sahil kept holding my hand the entire time. Niya whispered in my ear, "He confessed, right?" Before I could say anything, Sahil said, "I heard you, Niya, but your friend is yet to confess."

Niya made a small face and said, "Sahil, you will have to wait as you made her cry so much."

"I'm ready to wait my whole life," he said and kissed my hand, making me blush. All my pain and heartache evaporated like dew drops. Niya squeezed my other hand and said, "He is so romantic." This was the other side of Mr. Arrogant.

Karan and Niya took another table, giving us the desired privacy to talk.

Once we were left alone, I shed all my inhibitions and asked, "What is going on, Sahil?"

He raised an eyebrow and asked, "What do you mean?"

"What is the reason for this sudden change in your behaviour?"

He looked away as if gathering the right words, then said, "Anu, let me tell you all from the start. I have liked you from the very first day of our class together. Your innocence captivated me and I could sense after some time that you like me too. I enjoyed the way you got jealous and picked fights with me. When you hugged and kissed me the other day, I couldn't stop thinking about you the entire night like an insane person. I felt that if I didn't confess my feelings to you, I'd die of suffocation."

"But why did it take you so long to confess your feelings when you liked me?"

"I had to make some very difficult decisions before I came here. There are strict commitments holding me down. See, my father is a retired army officer and wanted me to join the army too. He agreed to let me pursue MBA on the condition that I would always remain in the top two of my class or else he would not pay my fees. For this reason, I was attending classes and following studies with a one-track mind. I didn't want to get involved in a relationship just for the sake of it or to pass the time, which is why it took me a long while to accept you as my girlfriend. I wanted to be sure that you are the right person for me. I don't want to hurt you. I have had a complicated past, Anu. I know how it hurts when you are in a wrong relationship."

"What about your mom? Does she support you?"

"My mother left my father for some other man when I was just three years old. When my father found out, he was devastated. It scarred him for life and turned him against love. When it was time for my brother to get married, he rejected the woman he loved and forced him to marry the girl of his choice alone. My brother agreed to the alliance but he was never happy, nor was he able he keep his wife happy. They were blessed with a beautiful girl a year later, but even she was not able to bind them together. As a result, my brother has now applied for divorce and is waiting for the proceedings. Their daughter, Reem, is very close to me as *bhai* does not have much time to spare for her. I don't want to undergo the same fate as my brother, but my father is adamant. That's why I was so afraid to acknowledge my feelings towards you."

"What made you confess now? As of last night, I had started hating you."

"Anu, I tried to sleep, but I was not able to. My heart bled at the sight of you crying. I wished to come flying to you to tell you how much I love you. I don't want to lose you. We will fight for our love together. I don't know what lies ahead of us, but I'm too weak to let you go."

I empathised with him over the pressure to perform well in studies. "Sahil, I want to be your strength and not your weakness," I said. "You call me a baby, but I must say that you are a baby who needs coaxing and pampering."

"Anu, you know, you are the only person who understood me so well in such less time."

I held Sahil's hand again and said, "Don't worry. I'm always here with you."

Niya and Karan interrupted us just then. "You two don't even look around when you talk. At least be mindful of who might be staring at you," said Karan.

Sahil smiled and said, "Your friend is so beautiful that I'm not able to take my eyes off of her."

"Aww, that's so sweet," said Niya pouting.

We returned back to our respective hostels after that, tired and full.

Niya jumped at the sight of Sahil's number flashing on my phone screen and said, "See, you used to tease me whenever Karan called. Now it's my turn."

I snatched the phone away from Niya and left the room as I knew she would have made me laugh while talking.

"Hey, you took so long to pick up my call," said Sahil.

"Niya was not giving me the phone," I replied. I heard him smirking behind his phone. "So, all good?"

"Yeah," he said, "All well. Why? Can't I call you without a reason?"

"Of course, you can call me anytime you want, Sahil."

"So, any plans for tomorrow?"

"None yet. Niya is going out with Karan so I thought I would take the chance to complete my pending work."

"Anu, would you like to go out with me to watch a movie tomorrow?"

I had always wanted to spend time with Sahil in my dreams, but when he actually asked me out, I did not know how to respond. I took my time, then said yes to him. Learning about the latest update the next day that I was going out with Sahil, Niya was eager to make decisions on what I should wear. She was determined to not let me wear my boring clothes. Like a lunatic, she turned my cupboard inside-out. All my clothes were dumped in a pile on my bed, making it look as if we had opened a quick sale at Janpath market. It took some time, but she finally picked out a floral print knee-length dress. I had once told her that I wanted to wear it on a special occasion.

"Here you go, Anu. The right time has come."

I genuinely wanted to look beautiful, but also did not want Sahil to feel that I had overworked myself like a mad woman in love. "No, Niya," I said, "This dress will be too uncomfortable for me." Sahil had never seen me in a dress like that.

"Anu, everybody wears these kind of dresses, and this particular dress is so beautiful. Sahil must know that you wear such kind of dresses so that he may not have any qualms about it later when you wear it. Otherwise, boys say, 'You never used to wear clothes like this before.'"

"Okay, Niya, you won the battle. I'm going to wear this dress."

Niya kissed me and said, "That's my little baby." I wore Niya's dress and my new pumps which I had bought from Delhi. I applied some slight kajal and a natural shade of balm on my lips. I tied the top half of my hair and put a clutch on it.

"You look so beautiful, Sahil will not be able to take his eyes off you, Anu," said Niya. "Good luck and have fun."

I ran down the stairs as Sahil had reached already and had called me twice. When I reached, he seemed to be a bit nervous like me, but when he saw me, he was awestruck by my appearance and kept looking at me with his beautiful eyes and charming smile.

"Anu, I did not realise you are so beautiful," he said and hugged me slightly. He was looking handsome as always in his black v-neck T-shirt and his favourite rugged jeans.

"You are looking good as always," I teased him.

He smiled and put his hand on my shoulder and said, "Lucky me. Let's be quick or else we will miss our movie."

We reached the PVR and while entering inside, I saw the name flashing sultan and before I could say anything, he pulled me into the darkness holding my hand. Sahil made me sit on the side corner seat and held my hand tightly. After a while a romantic track played in the movie and I held Sahil's upper biceps and rested my head on his shoulder and he brought his hand above my shoulder and pulling me towards him, he kissed my forehead and asked, "Are you enjoying the movie?"

I looked at his impeccable smile and said, "I'm enjoying your company," and kissed his dimples making him smile. Love makes you lose all your shyness, I have certainly not imagined myself kissing any boy ever and here I was deeply in love with this boy ready to do anything for his company. Sahil brought a large popcorn and one large coke during the break time, making me ask him where is my drink and he smiled and said, "I'm going to share it with you," and he made me blush. I have seen that in the movies and cursed the actors to do such kind of stupid and childlike scenes, and now I was sitting and was ready to do the same thing lovingly.

I took one sip and passed him the coke and then he took one sip and said to me, "Anu, I have not drunk such amazing coke before," and he made me blush again. It was an enthralling experience watching the movie with him and later we went to a close-by restaurant. He pulled the chair and made me sit on the chair and then he sat later. "Trying to be perfect gentlemen, haan?" I teased him and he said, "I'm a gentleman you should have no doubt by now."

He ordered a medium size pizza, and before eating he held my hand and, caressing my face with his other hand. He looked into my eyes and said,

"Thanks Anu for coming into my life and making it so worth living and when you are with me, I forget all my pain."

"Sahil, I cannot see you unhappy because..." I stopped.

"Because what, Anu? Are you still shy telling me those lovely words which I'm dying to hear from you? Remember, you are the first one to kiss me. Where is that bold girl of mine?"

I was so overwhelmed hearing this that it warmed my eyes. I held both his hands and said, "Sahil, I love you. I don't know how it happens, but I'm crazy about you and can't spend even one minute without you. You had made my life go upside down, please don't ever hurt me as my heart is not so strong to let you go."

Sahil wiped my tears and said, "Don't worry I'm always with you, my baby. By the way, from when were you preparing this speech?

I pushed him a little and he hugged me, and I found my solace in his strong arms.We walked back to my hostel and I was not ready to let him go, pulling him toward me, I hugged him tightly and this time he reciprocated with a tighter hug and I kissed him on his lips making him lose his ground.

He embarrassingly looked into my eye and said, "Anu, you are so unpredictable," and then he was standing there until I entered the gate; the protective side.

Niya was sitting with the bag full of questions which were thrown at me as soon as I entered, "So gorgeous, how was your first date?"

Unable to express my feelings I simply went and hugged her tightly. She hugged me back and said, "Oh my god Anu! You are smelling of him. What were you guys up to? I hope you did not do anything silly on your first date."

"Of course, no Niya, you know both of us personally."

"Yeah, I do, but boys are always boys," and then we started laughing and later I narrated her my evening.

I tried to sleep after this, but in vain, I tried switching off all the lights, keeping the pillow on my face like Niya, but still I was not able to sleep. He was there to bother me in my sleep as well. I was missing him for sure, I blushed just thinking of him in my room running his fingers in my hair with his soft hands and then kissing me on my forehead; the feeling was spellbound and soon I drifted to sleep dreaming about him.

Chapter 9

Niya had left early to attend her class and I was late as I was dreaming about him the whole night, cursing myself, I got ready and rushed towards the mess to have my breakfast, luckily I reached in time and quickly grabbed two idly and kept it in my lunch box and ran to the college. Mrs Iyer had started her class and she was infuriated when she saw me at the door, asking her permission to come in. Sahil gave me a scowling look, but Mrs Iyer look was more dramatic.

Miss Ananya, she started in her south Indian accent, if you had scored good marks in the class so it does not mean that you can come late to class.

I stuttered and said I'm sorry ma'am, it won't happen next time.

She let me come inside, making bad faces but I was happy to see Sahil sitting alone, so I made my way towards him, but it did not get down well with Mrs Iyer. She shouted, making me freeze and said ohh no girl you are not sitting with him, come and sit in the front row. I felt like killing her and telling her to stop being her mom but I controlled myself and sat in the front row. I was not able to pay attention to anything she taught. I sat like a blank person seething with revenge and immediately ran from the classroom after the class was over without confronting Sahil and Karan. I hate Mrs Iyer, or maybe she had a crush on my Sahil. The feeling of addressing him as my Sahil was so comforting that my anguish was melted for the love for him.

I was sitting on the stairs alone eating my idly when I saw Sahil and Karan giggling and coming towards me. Karan fell down the opposite side laughing while holding his stomach and Sahil sat in front of me and kissed my forehead and said Ananya, you are such a baby, when will you grow up.I'm not a baby, I snapped at Sahil and punched Karan oh his stomach and said what is there to laugh.

Sahil held my hand and said, Ananya first you came late and secondly, you were coming and sitting with me.

I pulled my hand from his hand and said so what; it is my choice where ever I sit.Sahil gave me a darning look and then his lips curved into a smile.Anu you know how possessive she is about Sahil said Karan.

Ok, Sahil then why don't you go and ask her out, and I picked up my lunch box and came back to the class, leaving behind both of them laughing.

I sat on the first bench and opened my book.

hi Anu how are you said Bhavika startling me and where is your handsome boyfriend?

I'm fine Bhavika and its none of your business.

Oh, so finally you are accepting that he is your boyfriend,You were before him from the first day itself and showing that you are not interested in him.You small town girls are very clever; you know how to trap boys from good families.

I stood up in anger and was about to say something, but Sahil was there for my rescue and he did not give me the time to say anything.

"How dare you Bhavika?" I know very well who was after me for what reason, there is no need for you to tell me. Apologize to Ananya right now."

Sahil's eyes were raging with anger and his stern look made Bhavika tremble and she immediately murmured a sorry and went out of the class but when she saw Ronan coming she started crying more and said something in his ear. I was scared and did not want a big fight between Sahil and Ronan, as they were about to fight the last time as well. Seeing Bhavika crying Ronan folded his shirt up from his arm and came towards Sahil, who also folded his shirt sleeves up.

Karan stepped in between Sahil and Ronan, but he was pushed aside by both of them.

What is happening in my class shouted Mrs Iyer seeing both of them, holding each other's collars. Mrs Iyer was fuming with anger and looked at Sahil who bowed his head down.

"Sahil! I want to talk to you in my cabin right now," she shouted and walked out of the class. Sahil looked at me and walked out leaving me standing like a statue all pale and frightened. Thank god Mrs Iyer forgot her specs in the class and came back to take it and saved Sahil from the dirty fight.

Sahil did not came back to attend the class and I thought to give him a little time to recover before I talk to him but when I went out he was nowhere. I saw Karan standing near the café along with Niya with a worried expression. I could see distress in Niya's eyes and my heart gave a jolt looking at her. "Where is Sahil?" I asked Niya.

"He had gone back to the hostel," Said Karan looking worried.

Karan was quiet and looking fidgety as if he was hiding something. I held his hand and said, "Karan, look into my eyes and tell me what did he say?" Karan gulped as if it was difficult for him to say it. "Karan, what happened, why are you not telling me?"

"Sahil said he doesn't want to talk to you anymore and you should maintain distance from him, as you are affecting him and distracting him from his studies which are more important to him." I felt like somebody had taken my heart out and broken it into small pieces and then asked me to breathe.

"But Karan what did I do? What happened all of a sudden?" My voice was choking. I was not able to speak up and tears started welling showing the pain which was within me.

"Oh Ananya!" Said Niya hugging me, "I told you not to get too attached to him. His studies are more important to him. Karan why did you not stop him?" "I tried to Anu, but you know how he is. I guess Mrs Iyer said something to him." Niya took my hand and said, "Lets go to our hostel, let that loner stay alone." "Niya I love him, his pain is mine now. I just wanted to know what made him so upset, that he did not even attend his class."

No need to think about him, Niya scolded me and dragged and me to the hostel. I was feeling so desolate, without him. Sahil had occupied a special place in my heart in a very short span of time. I was feeling emptiness within myself; something was pricking my heart again and again making me cry all the time. I wanted to talk to him but restrained myself as I knew he will not pick up the phone and that will make me cry more. Falling in love with somebody is so easy, it's the best feeling in the world, but heartbreak is so difficult, it's the worst feeling in the world. I cried the whole day but then I gathered myself and thought about the purpose for coming here and about my parents, and for nobody in this world, would I make my parents suffer. It's good it all ended so soon barring me the pain which I must have faced later on, as I knew Sahil's father was against love marriage.

The next day I woke up without crying, the pain was still lingering within me and wanted to show its way out through my eyes, but I was strong enough to stop it and I had to be brave in order to face him.

I was happy to see Karan waiting for me at the college gate but he

still held that worried expression seeing me. I smiled and assured him that I was ok. Niya and Karan were my pillars of strength. I was lucky to have friends like them.

Sahil was nowhere to be seen, but he made his way slowly after Mrs. Iyer entered and went straight to his favourite old seat at the back without even looking at me. It pricked me really hard, but Karan closed his hand over mine tightly making me stable. Sahil had a very weary expression on his face, his eyes were red as if he had not slept for the entire night or cried. I dismissed the feeling immediately thinking he would not cry for me. A cold hearted person back in his old form, without a trace of smile on his face. Mrs Iyer was happy to see both of us not sitting together and Bhavika was brimming with happiness.

Mrs. Iyer flashed all her yellowish teeth and commented before going.

"Sahil good to see you back to your den looking towards me," I felt like throwing my pen on her face. Sahil did not say anything and rather faced the other side, exactly the way he used to do before. As soon as

Mrs. Iyer went, Rustogi sir came with papers in his hands announcing the second term examination

Before leaving the class I looked at Sahil and for once he also looked at me and the message was clear to him, that I'm not going to spare him this time and will top the class.

I buried myself in my books and decided to fight tooth and nail to come first. I had stopped going out or eating much making Niya always worried about me and running behind me for food. Sahil did not speak to me or call me anytime before the exam, neither did I bother to think about him.

Our exams started soon after and we made it a point not to bump into each other, or changed directions if we ever came the same way. I had completely banned his thoughts to come inside my mind. Days passed by quickly bringing an end to our second semester and promoted us to our second year marking an end to the first year leaving me with good and bad memories.

Chapter 10

The first sunday after the exam and my birthday came together. I waited next to my phone till 1 in the night for Sahil's call, but he did not call. Though I had stopped talking to him, but still my heart wished that Sahil would call me. I just hated him in that moment, thinking did he ever love me even for a single minute? All those things which he told me were all illusion, was he passing his time with me? I dismissed his thoughts and said to myself you will know when the results are out and you will not top this time. Niya and Karan wished me first followed by my brother Aryan and my parents.

"Anu get ready fast. Karan is waiting for us downstairs." Shouted Niya.

"Please Niya, you know I'm feeling terrible. I don't feel like going anywhere."

"Anu please, I have planned so much for you, please don't ruin everything."

I didn't want to go but I also didn't want to spoil Niya's mood as she had done so much preparation to make my day. Niya forced me to wear a beautiful dress which she had brought for me as my birthday present. It was light pink in colour and had a broad black colour band on the waist giving it a very feminine look, divided in between which really made the dress look super cool. I tied my hair in half and applied some liner and lip gloss; not too bad a sight to look at I guess, except the occurrence of slight under eye circles due to studying and crying for him

Niya had worn a black halter neck top and short cream capri and she was looking fabulous. "Let's go Ananya!" she called me, standing outside the room. I was stopped by a phone call which was coming from an unknown number.

"Hello."

"Hi Ananya di, happy birthday."

It took me a second to realize that it was Reem.

"Thank you so much Reem. How are you and how do you know it's my birthday?"

"Sahil chachu was telling me from many days that your birthday is coming so I remember."

"Reem, does he know that you are calling me?"

"No di, chachu gave me your number long back and said that I can call you whenever I like."

"Oh, thank you so much Reem. You made my day."

"Ok bye di, take care of chachu."

"Sure Reem," I quipped without revealing our status further as she was too young to understand.

"So he knew my birthday, then why did he not wish me? What is going on in his mind? Why is he behaving like this?"

Niya called me again, breaking my thoughts and dragging me outside.

We took an auto from outside along with Karan and to my surprise Niya tightly hugged and kissed Karan getting him out of breath.

"Niya, I'm not able to breathe," said Karan looking embarrassed.

I remember when I had kissed Sahil in the café; he was horrified. Changing times I guess; women are being more outspoken about their relationship while guys are shying away.

Niya made a baby face and said, "I couldn't help myself. You are looking so cute."

He engulfed Niya in a tight embrace and whispered in her ear, "We can do this while we play bowling."

"I heard that," I said it with a smile getting the three of us to giggle. I was missing my Sahil, no, not *my* Sahil anymore. I imagined him cuddling me on my forehead, which used to give me so much solace. I was missing him for his strong arms around me and his cute smile.

We reached a beautiful restaurant which was famous with the youngsters as the ambience was mesmerising and there was desired privacy for couples in love. Karan and Niya had already come here a lot many times and it was nothing new for both of them as they belonged to big metro cities and had seen this before. It was me who was feeling out of the world. The ambience was beautiful with soft lights of different colours glowing everywhere, the music was so loud that it was making it difficult for us to listen to each other and then there were separate small cubicles made to give some privacy to the couples madly in love. I was feeling out of place now as I felt I was ruining Niya and Karan's day. I kept missing Sahil.

Had he been here, I would have placed my head on his shoulder and would had lost myself .

"Ananya will you sit or continue staring at this place?" Karan shouted in my ear..Niya held my hand and asked, "Nice place na?"

She sensed my feelings and said, "You are missing him."

My eyes welled up with tears. She raised her hand to wipe them but I stopped her before it reached my cheek, smiled and said, "I wish he was hear Niya. I'm missing him so much and he did not even wish me today."

Niya hugged me tight and said, "Ananya, you are a lucky girl. Sahil is head over heels in love with you."

I stared at her with wide eyes, wondering what made her say that.

Before I could ask her anything, Karan came in with a beautiful chocolate cake which was backed by dark brown chocolate.

"Wow Karan! But how did you know this is my favourite cake? Only Sahil knew about this." Niya and Karan smiled looking at me.

"Sahil has ordered this cake for you."

"What are you guys saying!?" And then I saw Sahil coming in making me still, so still that I was not able to take my eyes off him. He was looking mesmerizing in his white collar shirt, which he teamed up with army pants and black shoes, there was a slight stubble on his face, which was a little more from the last I remembered. He smiled. His beautiful dimpled smile which made me forget all my pain and agony. I just wanted to run and kiss his beautiful dimpled face, but I was still not able to move. Sahil came close to me and seeing me not getting up, he pulled me up gently from my shoulders and made me stand face to face so that I could see through his dark brown eyes what lay beneath.

He kissed me on my forehead and said, "Happy Birthday, baby. How did you think of cutting the cake without me?"

I was looking blankly towards him, expressionless. I was not able to express my happiness and then tears came trickling down my cheeks before I could not stop them. I could see his eyes also moisten a little, but he controlled. He wiped my tears and shook his head and then pulled me towards him and hugged me tight.

I held him back and forgot about the pain which I had gone through. I was numb to say anything to him. I just cried and buried myself in his chest and felt his soothing hands on my lower back, touching me softly. I held on tighter. I didn't want to let go of him even for a moment.

Niya coughed in the background and broke our moment. "Guys, we need to cut the cake and Ananya, you can ask Sahil everything later."

Even I did not feel like asking him anything as I wanted to enjoy the present moment. I cut the cake to everybody clapping and smiling and singing the birthday song.

'These three were my life. How would I have functioned without them?'

Sahil held my hand and said, "I'm sorry Anu for all the pain which you have gone through because of me but I was forced to stay away from you."

"What are you saying Sahil? Who forced you?"

"You remember Mrs. Iyer called me that day after the fight?"

"How can I forget that day Sahil. What did she say?"

"She said that I know Sahil you were fighting because of Ananya and you have also helped her in the assignments and I will not give her any marks in this assignment and when she will fail, she will come to know what it is like to distract people like you. I tried to explain to her that I have not helped you in doing her assignment but she was not ready to hear anything and said luck does not favour every time and I had no option except to do things her way.

So I took a U-turn and told her that I think she was right and even I didn't want to score less because of Ananya. and I will maintain a distance from you, but .. Ananya, she indirectly threatened me that she will not let you pass if I did not break my ties with you. It was very difficult for me, you know as I knew you would be very upset. I wanted you to be motivated to study hard and show her what you are really made up of."

Tears were flowing down my eyes. Sahil wiped my tears and said, "Please don't cry. I would not let anybody ruin your life because of me."

I looked up into his eyes and said, "I am sorry for doubting you." Sahil kissed me on my forehead and said, "Don't ever doubt my love for you again."

"Sorry Anu," Said Karan, "I knew about all this and I thought that Sahil was right in doing so. So I didn't tell you."

"Karan you knew it all the time and you never told me!"

"Because we both felt that you were not able to concentrate and we really wanted Mrs. Iyer to know how capable you are and in order to do that you had to study hard."

Sahil's phone buzzed at that moment. He was startled to see the number flashing on his mobile.

"My dad," he mouthed and went outside.

Karan turned towards me and said, "You know Anu, Sahil was so shaken by this incident that he literally cried for you and it was shocking to see him so emotional. And I remember how his eyes were red when he came to the class for the first time after saying that he will not talk to me anymore." Karan opened up to me about Sahil.

"He was as broken as you, seeing your condition. He did not sleep properly yesterday and was sitting with me when I called you yesterday for your birthday, and seeing you cry, he also got emotional and was on the verge of a break down and only I know how difficult it was for me to bring him back.

"Anu he loves you a lot, don't ever doubt his intention."

Tears refused to flow down my cheeks. I saw Niya also crying, "Oh Anu, he loves you so much. You are such a lucky girl!" We wiped our tears when we saw Sahil coming back. "Karan, why are you making these beautiful girls cry?" Sahil teased Karan.

"Everything all right?" I asked Sahil seeing his expression change.

Sahil gave me his smile and nodded. We ordered pizza and some pasta and had a fun evening.

After a while Niya gestured Karan to get up. As he was getting up, I asked, "Where you guys are going?"

Niya scowled and said she wanted to spend some time alone with her boyfriend.

"But we have all come together," I tried to argue. Sahil smiled and looked the other way.

"Oh ho Anu, grow up and don't be so dumb. You are not alone. Sahil is there with you."

That was my worst fear, sitting alone with Sahil. Although we had met before as well but not at a place which was so private. Moreover now there had been a gap between us when we were not talking, bringing that strange feeling back again

It was like starting all over again.

Sahil held my hand and said, "Relax, let them go. I'm here with you." I gave him a half hearted smile and nodded.

Niya came close to me and said, "He is all yours now, and you can do whatever you feel like. At least kiss him proper."

She winked at me leaving me shocked. I glanced slightly at Sahil and saw him grinning.

Sahil stood up and sat next to me making my heart beat doubly fast till he kept his hand over my shoulder pulling me into his soft embrace. He said, "I'm sorry for what I had done. Please forgive me."

I could only shake my head without looking towards him. He looked at me and I could see appreciation in his eyes, saying, "Anu you are looking stunning today. I'm not able to take my eyes off you."

I blushed and said a meek thank you and then added, "You are also looking really good today."

He smiled and said, "Less than you, baby." We were looking at each other as there were no words left to express our feelings.

Finally, I waved off my naïve and shy self and I shifted closer to him, removing any distance and put my head on his shoulder and caressed his cheek with my fingers. He was immobile for a moment and I could hear his heart beat accelerating with an enormous speed.

"Ananya," He said in a husky voice, "You are making me uncomfortable."

I raised my head slowly from his shoulder and looked into his eye, should I sit on the other side then.

Sahil clutched my back tighter and lifted me up on his lap and hugged me. His cheeks caressed mine and he said, "No baby, don't go anywhere. I'm liking it." Making me blush again. We both were looking into each other's eyes, as thousands of emotions flowed. I was close to him and could hear him breathe. Intoxicated with his fragrance, I was no longer feeling shy.

Sahil held my face and brought it down closer to him. He kissed me on my forehead and then on both my cheeks. The feeling was inquisite.

I didn't want him to stop and was ready to take my relation another step forward. He then kissed the corner of my mouth, making me lunge for more.

He looked into my eyes with love and passion and it was difficult for me to control, as I knew he was not going to take the first step being the gentleman that he was. I kissed him on his lips softly taking his breath away. He was so shy that he was not able to even look into my eyes. I lifted his face to mine and reached for his lips again and brushed my lips slightly against his lips and then kissed him softly, feeling our love for each other. He clutched my lower back tightly with his hands. I was enjoying his strong arms encircling me as if I meant the world to him. I could sense his eagerness. We were so into it that our tongues met slightly and then his was exploring my whole mouth saviously, sending shivers down to my whole body. All our love and emotions were poured into each other in our first kiss.

He then looked into my eyes and said, "Anu, I love you so much."

"I love you too Sahil," We both were so engrossed that we did not see Karan and Niya standing and staring at both of us.

We were frozen, not able to look towards them.

Niya sat beside me and said seriously, "Anu, I just asked you to kiss him slightly and look at you guys! You just broke the record!" She teased me making me blush, then she punched Karan on his arm and said, "Learn something from Sahil," making him turn red in his face with embarrassment, "You never kissed me like this Karan."

"Oh Niya, don't worry, I will practice it with him," Making all of us laugh hard. It was one of the best birthdays I had celebrated ever.

I was holding Sahil's hand in the auto all the way back to the hostel. He was feeling sleepy on the way, his head hanging every now and then, making me giggle.

I kissed him on his cheeks out of sheer affection and rested my head on his shoulder. They dropped us first but I was not ready to leave him. Niya somehow managed to drag me to our room.

Without changing my dress I jumped on my bed and was soon lost dreaming about him. His soft touch was still embedded within me as I was madly in love. He was mine and I was ready to do anything or pass any test to make him mine forever. Niya came back from the washroom squealing at me to change my dress and stop thinking about him. I got up unwilingly and made my way to the washroom.

Chapter 11

We had decided that we will not sit together in front of Mrs. Iyer and would not talk to each other to avoid others' attention. This was the only way we could avert her attention and not let her interfere with my academics, though it was very distracting to not look at my love sitting just inches away from me.

It was Mrs. Iyer's class and Sahil was sitting on the last bench and Karan beside me. After a few minutes I glanced towards Sahil when Mrs. Iyer was busy writing something on the board and loved watching him engrossed in taking down notes. He was more serious about his studies than me. Maybe it stemed from the fear of his father or maybe he wanted to prove something to the world. There was a lot to know about him, all I knew was that I loved him dearly and was ready to do anything for him

Karan shook my hand and broke my day dreaming and said, "Ananya, stop looking at him. She will throw you out." I came back to my senses, but every chance I got, I looked towards him and this time I caught him looking towards me and signalled me to pay attention to the board. How could I pay attention when he was so close to me! Our relationship had become more intimate after sharing that kiss and I longed to be in his arms always.

Mrs Iyes left the class leaving us with our results displayed on the board and I knew I topped because he pushed me to do that, but competing with my love was sheer stupidity. I knew his dad would be mad at him and may threaten him with not giving him any money. Oh God, how was I thinking of hurting him while he was doing everything for me? Sahil came towards me and tears came down my eyes running a marathon race from my eyes. Sahil gave me a small hug and said, "Hey baby, why are you crying? You proved her wrong. I'm so proud of you."

We were in the second year and ready to take up specialization. Sahil, Karan and I opted for finance. The reason was not love and friendship here for the selection, but luckily we three were more interested in the financial aspects of business. Niya took Human Resource as she was perfectly suited for that with her probing and calculative nature. Our lessons had started off with great speed owing to the vast syllabus and we all were deadly piled up with back to back assignments, unit tests and presentations, leaving us all drained and tired, but today was a special day, as it was Niya's birthday and she decided to give her birthday party at a disc.

"Niya, I had never been to a disc before, what will I do there?"

"Oh come on Ananya, you dance so well, you can dance and why are you so scared? Karan and Sahil are there with us."

"But still Niya..."

"Anu stop your drama!" She threw a light cream colour sleeveless top with frills and a short black tight fitting skirt at me, "Go now and wear this."

"Niya I can't wear this. It is too short."

Niya came and kept her hand on my shoulder and said, "Anu you will look out of place if you wear long dresses. We are not going to a beach."

She made a baby face and pleaded, "Please for me... it's my birthday."

I sighed, losing my battle as always. Niya wore a neon bodycon with her new high heels and was looking stunning like a diva.

"Whoa Ananya! You are looking awesome!" Said Niya and forced me to apply some foundation and mascara.

She got me to look into the mirror. I was bemused to see myself looking so different, the ordinary girl from a small town was looking like an up-town girl.

We made our way downstairs and became the victim of girls' scorching eyes, who were eyeing us up and down, especially me, as they had never seen me before like this.

Sahil and Karan were waiting outside. Karan was wearing a sleeveless vest and shorts and Sahil had his khaki capri and white t-shirt on.

He looked at me me minutely from head to toe and I could make out that he was not so happy with my clothes. Karan gave Niya a tight hug and kissed her on her cheeks and looked at me but said nothing. I guess he too sensed Sahil's feelings. I expected the same from Sahil to come and hug me, but he stood there still and slowly made his way to me and without a trace of smile on his face he said in a firm and angry tone, "What the hell are you wearing Ananya?" making me shiver like a baby. "What is wrong with the dress?"

"She is looking so beautiful, why are you spoiling my birthday?" Niya helped.

Sahil gave Niya a disapproving glance. Karan pulled her away. He knew better than to speak between a couple. "I was not able to look into Sahil's eyes.

"Ananya don't try to be someone you are not and if you love me, please go and change your dress. I will not go with you like this. I'm possessive about the person I love and would not like other idiots staring at you. Wear something decent; it's not always necessary to bare your legs," He said, looking at Niya. Niya wanted to interrupt but Karan stopped her.

I quickly made my way back to my room with a tinge of guilt and changed from my skirt to my jeans without changing my top and made my way downstairs. Sahil came towards me and engulfed me in his arms and said, "I'm sorry but your dress was not good at all." He looked into my eyes and said, "Ananya, I love you for your innocence and your simplicity, please don't change yourself. You look so beautiful when you are not wearing any makeup, don't smear your beautiful face with these false things."

Karan coughed in the background and said, "He is right, you don't need all these things as you are a natural beauty," and then he glanced towards Niya, and she also got the message that Karan was not too impressed with her as well. There was stony silence in the auto. Sahil was sitting with the driver. Niya was engrossed in her mobile while Karan looked the other way. I felt really sorry for Niya, for spoiling her birthday. "Niya, I'm so sorry," I broke the ice, making everybody wonder what happened. She looked at me questioningly. "I forgot your gift in the room." She smiled and put her hand on my shoulder and forgave me for the error. I looked at Karan and asked, "So Karan what did you bring for Niya?"

Karan looked at Niya for a second and then embraced her in a tight hug and said, "I have brought a special gift for my princess," and then he kissed her. "Hey, don't you start to cry now. Let's enjoy your birthday!" Sahil was watching all this from the front. He said, "I'm so sorry for spoiling your mood. I should not have come to your party I guess." Niya placed her hand on his shoulder and said, "Don't spoil Ananya's mood now. I can understand. I should not have forced my choices on her. She did not even want to wear it. I forced her.

"Niya please, you are my friend and you have all the right over me."

She hugged me and said, "Yes, my baby, now forget everything and let's enjoy."

The auto stopped with a jerk as we reached our destination. 'Eccentric disc' was written in bold red letters. As we reached near the entrance I could hear loud noises. Sahil held my hand and whispered in my ear, "Don't go anywhere without me, not even to the washroom. I will accompany you," making me blush. Karan held Niya from her shoulders and there we were in a totally new world, which was non existent for me till now. The ambience was darkish with dim lights. Intermittently, lots of yellow fairy lights would glam the place to let it go back to the soft hues of before. The music was too loud to handle and there were large tables at the corners and behind the tables there was a small mini bar for drinks and juices. The tables were teamed up with high sleek revolving purple chairs and in the right corner I could see a board with a sign that the seating arrangement was upside. The dance floor was very big, I could see youngsters wearing dresses which were quite short and were dancing consistently. I could see some of the boys and girls on those high sleek chairs enjoying their drinks. I made my grip tight on Sahil's hand and he understood my inhibition. He enveloped me in his arms and said, "Don't worry, I'm with you."

Niya and Karan were ahead of us. She turned back and said, "We will go up and cut the cake." I gave her a half smile and we reached up. I could see drunk girls sitting, wearing really short dresses with their boyfriends or whoever they were. Thank God I was wearing my jeans. We took a place on the sofa in the corner. Niya's eyes were twinkling with excitement now, I knew she was enjoying but seeing my worried expression she said, "Anu just forget about the people here just think about you and Sahil." I could only reciprocate with a meek smile.

. Niya cut the chocolate cake with a childlike excitement and then placed a small piece in Karan's mouth and kissed him. Karan did not take even a moment to reciprocate making Sahil and me look the other side.

Niya broke the kiss and looked towards us and said, "You guys can also kiss, we had witnessed a good kiss the previous time." Sahil gave Niya a horrifying look and then she smiled and said, "Relax guys I was just joking," and then she got all excited about getting us on the dance floor. I looked nervously towards Sahil and he gave me his assuring warm smile. "Anu, don't worry," said Karan, "They are going to play soft numbers and we can dance a little for our birthday girl." Sahil held my hand and all four of us were on the dance floor. Sahil placed my hands on his shoulders and his hands slightly on my waist and then we were far away from that dance floor looking into each other's eyes and swinging slowly with the song. He then took my right hand and swirled me around twice, making me smile and then pulled me towards him and hugged me tightly planting a small kiss on my head.

The feeling was out of the world and I wanted the moment to freeze there so that the lovely feeling can sink into but all good things come to an end and so did ours. Sahil and I left for the hostel and Niya and Karan stayed back as they had other plans. Sahil kissed me on my cheeks before leaving me at the hostel and I slept dreaming about him. Niya came around 8 in the morning giving me her shy smile and clinged to me saying, "I love Karan so much!"

I knew at once what had transpired. I was aghast. "But Niya, don't you think that you guys should have waited until marriage? Niya suppressed her smile and said, "Anu, we both are ok with it. It is better to know your physical compatibility before otherwise it may lead to problems later, and we know that we are going to get married eventually. I have no regrets. This was the best birthday for me.

"Ok, tell me one thing did Sahil ever asked you to…"

"No, he did not," I replied before her sentence got complete.

"Wow, he is old fashioned."

"Thank God, he is old fashioned, Niya."

Niya smiled and said, "Hmmm, you guys are perfectly made for each other."

We were still not talking much in college to avoid any attention and especially to avoid Mrs. Iyer, who was still teaching us one common subject - Finance was a lot more to study and we got busy making our presentations and assignments, in order to be accurate in our calculations we had to practise lots of exercise, not leaving much time to talk to each other. We talked for half hour daily discussing about our class assignments and used to meet out on Saturdays and Sundays along with Karan and Niya.

Time flew adopting wings and we got busy with our placements and final examinations giving us less time to spend with each other. Our placements went smooth luckily placing all of us in the same city and to begin a new life but destiny had other plans.

Finally the day came for which we all had waited impatiently—Our Convocation day. Sahil had to go back to Bangalore immediately after the last exam . I waited for Sahil on the convocation day along with my parents, whom I had convinced about Sahil somehow, to lay a step forward for our relationship with best hopes and plans for the future but my Sahil did not come on that day breaking all my dreams and hope, leaving me alone forever.

FIVE YEARS LATER

Chapter 12

FIVE YEARS LATER

I sat in my cubicle, frowning at the reports that my team of five, three girls and two boys, had prepared.

"Zoya, what have you done? You seem to have lost all interest in your work." I looked Zoya in the eye, and then at Vikram, the boy she found unable to resist. "Zoya, nothing is more important than work, do you understand? You are paid a hefty amount to complete your work properly." She made a face, picked up her report and walked out, cursing me. "As for the rest of you, keep your reports here and I will go through them." Vikram gave me a sharp look, and I knew why. I had hurt his girlfriend. I knew that they were head over heels in love with each other, but I felt sorry for her, or perhaps jealous to see both of them in love like that. "You may leave now, please," I shouted.

My team hated me for my strict nature, but this is what I was there for. I had been appointed as a finance trainee five years prior by one of the biggest finance firms in the country and had worked hard day and night to get promoted to a managerial position where I handled a team of five trainees who knew nothing and were reluctant to learn anything new. I took a deep breath and walked out to get a coffee and clear my mind off the mess that the trainees had created.

On reaching the coffee station, I saw my trainees standing huddled around a tables like honey-bees. Upon reaching closer, I found that they all were consoling Zoya who was crying like a baby. Vikram was holding her hand, sitting beside her on the table. I could sense other people peeping from over their work stations, giving me weird looks. 'Yes, look at me, morons!' I yelled in my head. 'As if I am the most heartless manager here.'

Kavya, who headed the operations team, came out of her cubicle, looked at the group of my trainees and then at me. "Ananya, it seems as if you love calling trouble to your side," she said, giving me one of her sarcastic smiles. She was all tall with coloured hair and a beautiful hour-glass figure, a wicked smile and awesome interpersonal skills, and I hated her. Kavya walked upto the group, placated everyone to return to their seats and wiped away Zoya's tears. In only a minute, I could see a toothy grin on her face. I wondered sometimes why I was incapable of the diplomacy and shrewdness that Kavya had and control my trainees by myself. Vikram gave me a look of disgust. It was my cue to leave as I didn't want Kavya to return and be at the receiving end of her taunts again. She didn't have a particular liking for me either.

Kavya was a little jealous of me as she had been keen to head the finance department, but lacked the core knowledge for it. Through her shrewdness, she had managed to lead the operations department really well. All her trainees remained in awe of her, perhaps because of her looks or perhaps smooth words. I headed straight back to my cubicle without taking my coffee and sat down heavily on my chair. My heart went out for Zoya. I felt bad for scolding her, but it was due. She had been a dedicated trainee before Vikram joined, and I didn't want the poor girl to get distracted or lose her senses, as I did, if and when Vikram would leave her. I wanted to protect her from the clutches of his infatuation so that she wouldn't end up heartbroken as I had. Sahil's departure had left me devastated and broken. I dismissed the thought of him at once. It had taken me a long time to overcome the grief of him leaving me after the last day of college. He did not come back ever. I was lifeless without him. All my effort to contact him had been in vain. I was terribly shaken and felt as if my life had come to an end. Even my parents cried and cursed Sahil upon knowing about him, then cursed themselves for having sent me to Delhi. Seeing my parents' dream shattered, I resolved my dilemma and decided to come back to Delhi. My parents were in no mood to send me back, but after my pleading a lot, they decided to give me a second chance. I threw myself in my work so much that I hardly got any time to think about Sahil. I had only my work life, and no personal life, as I lost interest and trust in everybody. My mother was always worried about me and forced me to get married, but I had no interest in it as I knew I would not be able to love that person, and I didn't want to ruin his life. Everything was broken within me. All I knew now was my work.

I literally jumped from my seat as my phone rang, bringing me back to the present. I picked up the call and was received with a shrill voice, "In my cabin, Ananya, right now!" Manoj, the senior manager to whom I was reporting, was shouting like a manic. I knew it was the work of Kavya. She had to have complained about me and Manoj, so captivated by her looks, was not able to say no to that stupid Kavya. 'Why can't the bitch mind her own damn business?' I wondered. I knocked at his door and entered. Manoj gave me an annoyed look and asked me to sit. He seemed to be in a terrible mood, ready to attack. "Ananya, why are you like this?" I raised my brow quizzically at his words. "Why are you so cold and distinct with the employees?" I opened my mouth in an attempt to respond, but he waved his hands to shut me up. "I'm not finished yet, Ananya. Every month, there is a new complaint about you. I know you are a devoted and hard working manager, but you need to be a little empathetic towards your trainees and your colleagues. You don't mix up with anybody. I have not seen you talking and laughing with the others. What the hell is your problem? You lack interpersonal skills which are important for your position."

It was not something I had not heard before. Rather, it had become a habit for me to receive Manoj's lectures on the importance of interpersonal skills after somebody had complained about me. I knew Manoj was more inclined towards Kavya because of her looks, but he didn't want to lose a hard-working employee like me either who was always ready to take on new projects and was ready to work even on Saturdays and Sundays from home, so he always tolerated me. Manoj was an MBA from a top college and had been with the company for the past fifteen years, looking after all the departments. He was blessed with a rotund belly and eyes bulging out of his round chubby face. "Look, Ananya, I cannot save you from the management every time. You have gained a bad reputation in their eyes and it can hamper your growth." This was new information and made me a little pale as the promotions were due and I had really worked hard to get promoted.

Squinting his eyes, he looked at me and said, "You need to attend a counselling session with our team."

"What?" I gasped in horror. "Manoj sir, I'm not depressed or stressed out. Those trainees had not made their reports properly, that's why I lost my nerve with them. As you know very well, I don't tolerate nonsense with work."

"Ananya, you need to chill out a bit." He twisted his lips in a crooked smile then and said, "We have not kept counsellors here for depressed people, but to help employees work on their interpersonal skills and in dealing with stress."

I knew of one counsellor who was a doctor and helped employees in combating day-to-day stress. "Don't worry, I'm not sending you to him alone. Rather, it will be a workshop for all the employees working at a managerial position. We need to give some work to the poor counsellor as well. Now go and let me finish my work."

"Thank you, Manoj."

Later that day, the information about the counselling session was displayed on the boards. I went back to my cubicle to go through all the trainee reports. Rejecting them all, I picked them up, went to my team and threw them on the table, and said, "I want a revised report from all of you by tomorrow," and turned on my heels to leave. I could hear them muttering something about me in disgust.

I drove back and reached my flat by 7 PM. I had managed to buy a car by saving money over these last five years. I knocked on the door and Richa opened it, but rushed back quickly to our shared room. I knew she would be chatting with her boyfriend, Summit, on Skype as he had gone on a company project to Austin. I kept my bag on the table and went straight to the washroom. I wanted to be alone very much, but my mother's constant worry had made me stay with a room partner.

Richa was a fine looking girl with round eyes and a chattering mouth. She reminded me of Niya very much. I missed Niya a lot, but the distance and our work schedules had somehow caused us to drift apart. I had stopped talking to Karan as he was still friends with Sahil and was placed in the same company with him. I had even changed my phone number because I felt betrayed by them. I had no news of the three of them, nor they had any about me.

Richa knocked hard on the bathroom door and shouted, "Ananya, will you come out?"

I cursed myself yet again for not staying alone. "Yeah, in a minute."

"So, how was your day?" asked Richa, munching on a slice of pizza.

"It was nice. Everybody blamed me for my lack of interpersonal skills."

Richa began giggling. "Finally, they found out how you really are."

"Excuse me, what do you mean?"

"They are right, Ananya. You don't have a life of your own. You need to have a boyfriend and enjoy your life. Summit has many single friends. If you want, he can introduce you to some."

"So that they can break my heart and leave later?" I retaliated.

Richa made a face and said, "Ananya, not all boys are the same. Please, let go of your past, then only will you be happy. Sahil got married and moved on. What are you waiting for? Life is always about taking another chance."

She was right and her words pierced straight through my heart. Sahil was indeed married to some woman and, I assumed, was enjoying his life. And here I was living a dreadful life, heartbroken and cold.

He had moved on so easily, without thinking twice about me. All that he said to me had been a lie. That moron did not even have the guts to tell me that he was breaking off with me. Rather, he decide to disappear and abandon me. I didn't want my thoughts to linger upon his marriage, so I asked Richa about Summit and she was all smiles and blushes.

"He is good. He is returning next month, and then we will get married."

"Wow, Richa. That's great news, and you are telling me now!"

She came closer to me and said, "Ananya, I will miss you. It's high time you settle down too."

Richa was quite irritating at times, but the thought of her leaving was not entirely comforting. She never allowed me to ponder upon my past too much. I hugged her and said, "Don't worry, I will be fine."

Chapter 13

I woke up at seven the next morning and got ready for office as I needed to reach there by eight for the important meeting regarding the company's and the employees' grievances.

It was compulsory to attend for all the managers. I was getting ready when I received a call from my mother.

"Hey Ananya, how are you?" she asked.

"Mom, I'm getting late. Please, I will talk to you later."

"Ananya, listen. I found a match for you on shadi.com and you need to go and meet the boy this evening. He is an engineer."

"What?" I panicked. "Mom, what nonsense is this?"

"Ananya, how long do you plan to remain alone, crying after that stupid boy?"

My mom had gained expertise in searching for grooms for me, and I had gained expertise in making them run away. It was no use arguing with her, so I said,

"Okay, mom. Just SMS me his number and I will talk to him."

"Ananya, don't mess it up this time. He is a really nice guy."

"How do you know he is a really nice guy just by looking at his picture and the vitals he might have mentioned on the site? Half of the information people put there is fake." I heaved a deep sigh and entered my car.

I reached office just in time, only to find Kavya looking elegant in her tight trousers and an off-white shirt. She had left her hair loose over her shoulders. It was a perfect sight to look at. I, on the other hand, was wearing ill-fitted trousers and a shirt, paired with my flats, and my hair scrunched into a tight pony-tail and not a trace of makeup on my face. It made me look like the most dull person of all, but I never minded, pacifying myself with an I-don't-care attitude.

Manoj signalled me to sit down and the meeting started with a discussion of all the grievances in the company. It took them a whole hour to discuss the same topic again and again without a conclusion in sight. Finally, the vice-president stood up and said, "I heard about the counselling session for all the managers, and I think it is a very good idea. Before the appraisals, it will be good to know your shortcomings and work on them. One more thing, I would like to inform you all that some managers from our office will be sent to the Bangalore branch of our company for three months as that branch is incurring some losses in a certain division and our mangers here are efficient enough to take care of all the grievances there and correct the problem by providing good solutions."

I did not wish my name to be there, as I was in no mood to go to a new place.

"... and the accommodation will be provided by the company in a safe environment," said the vice-president with a smile on his face.

Back in my cabin, I went through the fresh reports of my trainees and was happy to find that they had indeed worked hard this time.

I called them in and said, "Very good and well done, guys. I expect the same from you every time, and Zoya, I'm sorry if I hurt you."

She, along with the others, looked at me in shock. "Don't stare at me, girl. I'm not as stoned-hearted as you might think." She smiled and said, "It's okay, ma'am," and they left with smiles on their faces.

'This was not that tough,' I thought to myself, but the toughest part of the day was yet to come. It was time for the counselling session to happen. 'Oh, crap! What would he ask?' I wondered. I knew he was good-looking and the biggest womanizer by what I had heard about him. I wondered why companies hired such jerks to waste their money on.

I reached his office and saw Kavya walking out, all blushes and smiles. She never left a chance to flatter, that's why she was dressed like that today.

She fluttered her eyelashes at me and said, "Oh God, the counsellor is going to die of boredom."

I mouthed 'get lost' at her, making sure that she heard it.

I knocked and entered the room, but there was nobody there.

"Miss Bhatia, you may sit. I will be right back," the counsellor called out to me from the adjoining room. His table was neat and clean with only a notepad, a pen, a small calendar with important dates marked with red, and a small name-plate with 'Ritvik' written on it.

He cleared his throat to draw me out of my thoughts. "Hi, Miss Ananya. How are you?"

"Hi, I'm fine, doctor," I said without smiling.

Ritvik was good looking, no doubt. He was not very tall, but had a fair complexion, sharp features, and a masculine jawline that made him look quite handsome. He was wearing a white coat over his light-blue shirt, and black trousers. He gave me a reassuring smile that caused dimples to appear on his cheeks and I felt captivated by his charm. His face looked so familiar. It took me only a second to realize that he looked like Sahil. 'God,' I cursed myself, 'Why am I still thinking about that jerk? He is still not out of my system.' Ritvik was fairer and a couple inches shorter than Sahil, but the resemblance otherwise was striking.

"Are you okay, Miss Ananya?" he asked, as I was still staring at him.

I swallowed audibly and said yes, still unable to take my eyes off him. He smiled and I felt as if I was just one of many girls for him who got tongue-tied by his charming appearance. Before he could get the wrong idea from me, I drew myself back to my senses and assumed a disinterested look.

"So, Miss Ananya, you have a problem mixing with people?"

"What!" I shrieked. "Who said that? It's not true at all," I said in a blunt tone.

"Oh," he said and smiled.

I wished I could tell him not to smile.

"Ananya, I have gone through your details and all I can tell you is that managers are not for themselves alone, but also for the people who work for them. Every now and then, they need to sort out their problems. If you do not take any interest in your team members, how will they discuss their issues with you? You need to be a little more empathetic towards your team members. Then only will you be a good manager. I know, working hard all day only to get a negative feedback is very disheartening, but you need to mix up with your team members more in order to get good results."

He smiled and said, "Is there anything in your past that has made you like this?"

'How dare he!' I thought. "Like what?" I asked in a disgusted tone.

"Oh, I'm sorry, Ananya, if I offended you, but I'm a psychiatrist and I can read faces. You can trust me and tell me."

"No, there is nothing." I was curt and he got my signal.

"Ananya, I just want to help you out, so please, don't make it so difficult for me. Manoj speaks so highly about your knowledge and I just want to help, that is why I'm appointed here."

'Why are these counsellors and HR people so annoying? They just want to extract information in the first go,' I thought.

"I think I am done here," I said and rose from my chair, making Ritvik frown.

He stood up too and said, "Now I'm damn sure, Ananya, that you are hiding something, and I'm going to find out very soon."

I didn't want him to acquire any wrong knowledge from other jealous sources, so I closed my eyes for a second and said, "I was dumped by my boyfriend whom I loved like crazy, so I threw myself into my work and expect the others to complete their work on time too. What's so wrong if I tell them to work properly? Are you happy now?"

His expression was unreadable. He stood shocked and bemused, then gave me a reassuring smile, captivating and beautiful.

"No, Ananya. There is nothing wrong in asking people to work. That's what you are here for. It's just that you need to follow a different approach and start trusting people as everyone is not the same."

"Thanks for your valuable time, doctor," I said and turned on my heels. He seemed deep in thought when I closed the door after exiting.

Thank god it is over, he was so damn irritating, but good looking, why he resembles so much to Sahil or it's just his dimples which are similar to him.I was distracted by him after a long time just because of his dimples.

After finishing my work, I remembered that I had to meet that boy from shaadi.com. He had messaged me the address and the time, and thankfully, it was near my office.

Cursing my mom, I went to the washroom to wash my face so that I might look fresh. I drove over to the venue, parked my car and asked him where he was.

He asked me to meet him in front of KFC. Slowly, I made my way upstairs. The place was full of youngsters hanging around, girls wearing beautiful short dresses, enjoying the company of their boyfriends and friends, giggling in their innocence and freedom.

I remembered my best pals, but they were not with me anymore. I was feeling out of place in my loose trousers and shirt, and my shitty flats. I could have brought something else to change into, but I really didn't want to look nice.

Somebody sitting in one corner of KFC waved at me. This guy must have recognized me from the picture on the website.

I smiled at him and sat down.

"Hi, I am Sooraj," he said.

He was short and dark with a broad face and a round nose over which sat his ugly spectacles.

"Hi," I said, thinking of running away from him.

"So, let me start with my introduction," he said, pushing his ugly spectacles up the bridge of his nose. "I'm an engineer and am currently working as a senior manager." His chest swelled with pride as if he was working for the Indian Army. "And you?"

"I work in finance," I replied uninterestedly.

"So Ananya," he started with a frown on his face, making him look more like a beast. "I will be frank with you regarding my expectations."

This was unbelievable! We hadn't even begun to get to know each other. "Yes, tell me," I said.

"My shift starts at six in the morning, so you will need to wake up a little early, around 5, depending on your skill in cooking. Also, you will have to take care of my ailing parents."

I felt exasperated upon hearing this and wanted to tell him off by asking him to hire a full time maid instead.

"Do you want me to work after marriage?" I asked.

He gave me a quizzical look. "Of course, I want you to work. I'm a liberal man. I don't want my wife sitting at home and watching those nonsense daily soap operas."

"It will not be possible for me to manage all the things alone. My job comes with a lot of pressure. I return home around 8 or 8.30, but we can hire a maid who can cook for us." I felt sure that I was not marrying this chauvinistic pig, but I wanted to test his limits still.

"Oh no, Ananya. My parents would never like to eat food made by a maid."

I felt like breaking his head. Men like these should let out an ad of wanting a full-time earning maid for the family.

Our talk was interrupted by a phone call he received and even his ringtone was as weird as him. He walked away to take his call.

I closed my eyes to think of how to get rid of this moron, and when I opened my eyes, I saw Ritvik standing in front of me.

"Hey, hi Ananya! I thought you didn't go out much. Nice to see you after office," he said.

"Hi, Ritvik. Yes, you are right. I don't go out much. I have come here to meet this guy for a prospective marriage."

"Are you kidding me?" he asked shocked. "Ananya, you came to meet a boy for marriage wearing these clothes?"

For a minute, I felt embarrassed about my clothes. After a long time, I felt as like I really needed to go shopping.

"What's wrong with my clothes? This is the real me," I said.

"Wow. Hats off, Ananya. You are a headstrong woman. Other women must have spent hours in front of the mirror to get dressed for a man."

"Thank God then that I'm wearing these clothes because this man is a jerk. All he wants is a house maid who earns."

Sooraj came back just then and stared at Ritvik, expecting an explanation about his presence.

Before he could ask anything from me, I said, "Sooraj, I just want to say that you are a good example of a male chauvinist who just needs a full-time maid to fulfil your expectations. You don't need a wife, you need a maid who will take care of all your tantrums. Secondly, when my boyfriend is so far good-looking and has no expectations from me, I would rather marry him than you."

Ritvik started laughing like a maniac, looking less like a counsellor and more like a young good-looking boy having a good time. He reminded me of Sahil, although he was less boisterous and enigmatic. But why was I comparing Ritvik with Sahil?

"Will you stop laughing, doctor?" I intervened as he was unable to control his laughter.

"I'm sorry, Ananya. I'm just in awe of you. You are really something."

"What do you mean?"

"When I met you for the first time, I thought you are a dull workaholic type of a girl, but you proved me wrong. You are a strong woman and I have really started admiring you now. You don't need a counsellor. In fact, you can counsel many other women who are not able to take a stand."

"I'm sorry for calling you my boyfriend," I said apologetically.

"The pleasure is all mine, Ananya," he said, giving me his most flirtatious smile.

I needed to move before he took a wrong hint. "Okay, doctor. I'm leaving now."

"What?" he frowned. "Why? Come have dinner with me and my friends."

"Oh no, Ritvik. I will not be comfortable, and I don't go out with anybody anyway."

"See, Ananya, that's your problem. I'm a doctor and I can tell that you have thrown yourself in work and are without any friends. I don't know about your past much, but you should change your future. You should go out more and make new friends. That is the way to improve your interpersonal skills," he said and winked at me.

When I did not budge, he said, "Ananya, you are a stubborn girl. Okay, I did you a favour by letting you call me your boyfriend, now I want my favour returned by you joining me for dinner."

I made a face and said, "Fine, I hope my clothes don't offend you."

"Come on, Ananya. I am least bothered by what you are wearing. You look great anyway."

It had been long since I heard somebody call me 'great'. Ritvik lead me to the corner of the restaurant where four of his friends were sitting cosily."

"Hey, guys. Meet my friend, Ananya."

Everybody gave me a warm smile and a generous welcome.

One of the girls said, "I have never met her before, Ritvik."

"She is a recent addition to my friend-list," Ritvik said, giving her his reassuring smile.

"Nice to meet you, Ananya."

"Same here" I responded.

We ordered our dinner and chatted like old pals.

They asked me questions and teased Ritvik, who only answered in giggles. I felt like my life had changed. Ritvik had been right; I needed to make more friends in order to forget about my past.

Ritvik and I bid them goodbye after dinner as they had other plans.

"So, Ananya, should I drop you home?"

I smiled and looked at him, "No, thank you. I will drive back."

"Ananya, you are an independent woman."

"That I am, and thank you so much. I really enjoyed every moment of this evening after a long time."

"Don't worry, Ananya. I will help you develop your interpersonal skills soon," he said and we laughed together.

Chapter 14

My mother called me up that night to ask about my meeting with Sooraj. "Mom, he was a jerk," I told her, putting an end to her fifteen minute long rant.

"Ananya, you don't want to get married. How much time do you need to move on, beta?"

"Mom, I'm going to Bangalore for three months as the branch there is facing losses," I lied to save myself, and secretly wished now to get a chance to go there. I promised my mom that once I got back, I would marry the boy of her choice. That momentarily put an end to her blabber.

"But Bangalore is so far, beta," she said.

"Don't worry, mom. It takes only two hours by plane."

"Okay, beta. Take care. I'm always worried."

"Okay, bye mom."

I reached office on time the next morning and, for the first time, I felt happy and light upon entering my office.

I was smiling while explaining the topics of research to my team, perhaps confusing them with my changed behaviour. During lunch time, I went and sat in one corner of the canteen, having my lunch alone as usual. Kavya always sat in the centre of the room with all the senior managers whom she flattered everyday, Manoj being one of them.

Suddenly, I saw Kavya and some other trainee girls whispering and blushing over something. Then, I saw Ritvik putting his food on his plate, giving his captivating smile to every woman around him. Kavya was trying hard to catch his attention. She shouted, "Hey, Ritvik, come and join us."

He smiled half-heartedly and said, "There is no place to sit." To my horror, I saw him coming towards me the next moment, making all the women and Manoj look at me in utter shock, as if I was the ugliest thing in the world.

"Hey, Ananya," he smiled at me his dimple clad smile. "How are you and why are you sitting alone?"

"I don't want to get bored sitting with them."

"Me too," he quipped, "Listening to all the detail about finance."

Chewing on a piece of carrot, he asked me, "So, are you free this evening?"

"Yes, why?"

"So we can go out for dinner together," he said, finishing his carrot.

"Ritvik, you are working too hard to develop my interpersonal skills."

"I'm a perfectionist in my job, Ananya," he said, making me smile.

"Not today, Sahil." I bit my tongue as soon as the words escaped my mouth.

He raised one eyebrow and said, "Sahil, han? Your ex-boyfriend?"

I just shook my head and said, "I'm sorry."

"It's okay, Ananya. You are still living in your past. Break-ups happen, but people move on. He is the most unlucky man on earth to have left a girl like you. Anyway, let's not talk about your past." When he saw me upset still, he said, "So, Miss Ananya, please join me for dinner on Wednesday as you will be leaving on Thursday for Bangalore."

"Wow, it's good to be friend with you. I get information before everybody else does," I said.

"Miss Ananya, I don't know why people call you a cold and boring person. For me, you are the funniest person with the most witty sense of humour I have ever come across."

"Ritvik, let me go now. Otherwise, the women who dote on you will die of heartaches."

He winked and said, "I'm use to it, Ananya."

On the display board, the names of all the mangers and trainees who were to go to Bangalore were mentioned. Kavya's name was there too along with the procurement and logistics managers.

I packed all my clothes in time. It was a relief to know that all the managers were to stay in the same guest house that belonged to a person who was at the same level of seniority as Manoj. He had offered to providing us accommodation in his guest house for free in order to help the company.

On Wednesday evening, I quickly changed into dark blue denims and an off-white top with flowers on it. I was going to meet Ritvik in the next half an hour and I didn't want to embarrass him again with my ill-fitted shabby office-wear.

I quickly made my way out of the room and was waiting for parking when Ritvik called.

"Hey Ananya, I'm waiting for you in front of KFC," he said, teasing me for my previous episode with that moron.

"I will be there in five minutes, sir," I said, grinning. Ritvik had a special quality of making me feel like my own age, I knew he was helping me as a friend to come out of my shell, but it could still seem otherwise to others, but I really didn't care anymore.

He was grinning when he saw me. He was looking more handsome today in his black jeans and a red and white plaid shirt.

I could feel him staring at me.

"Wow, Ananya, you look beautiful...except your hair," he muttered and smiled.

"Stop embarrassing me, Ritvik. I don't want you to feel awkward with me when I am in my office clothes."

"You look good in office clothes as well."

"Stop being a counsellor here who is trying to boost his patient's morale."

"So, you do accepted me as your doctor."

"Yeah, yeah, well, let's go and eat something. I have to wake up very early in the morning."

"Is that something difficult for you, Ananya?"

"Shut up, doctor."

One hour passed and we were still not finished with our talking.

"I will miss talking to you, Ananya, but don't worry, I will join you in Bangalore shortly to boost the morale of people who lack in interpersonal skills."

"Especially the women," I mouthed, looking the other way.

"Ananya, I'm not a ladies' man, as I believe in stability."

"Oh, I thought you were a womaniser."

"Why did you think of me that way?" He seemed hurt.

"Because I have heard girls fawning over you non-stop, but I was not aware that it's a part of your job to be sweet to others."

"Thank god, you know me now."

"Ritvik, I don't want people to get a wrong idea about us."

He was quiet for a moment, then curled his lips up in a smile and said, "Look, Ananya, I think we both enjoy each other's company and that is what matters the most, isn't it? In just a few days, you have become a good friend of mine and I like spending time with you as you are so different from other women, never trying to pretend."

Maybe he was right, I thought, and that I should not over-think it.

"So, what about your personal life?" I inquired.

"I am dating a girl, but right now we have maintained some distance to know for sure whether we are meant for each other or not."

I partly felt bad that he was engaged, but I was also relieved. I could continue being friend with him.

"What do you mean?" I asked.

"Ananya, I love her, no doubt, but there are so many issues between us regarding our future life that I need to have a clear mind when thinking about it."

"Like?" I coaxed him for more information.

"Like, she wants to move to the US and spend her life there, whereas I want to stay in my own country and do not like the idea of settling abroad, and there are many more issues. I will tell you all later. It's too late and you had to drive back home."

Bidding him goodbye, I reached home and collapsed on my bed. I woke up around seven the next morning and made my way to the washroom to get ready quickly.

Richa hugged me tightly with tears in her eyes. I wanted to tell her that it was only an escape route from my mother and I would be back after three months.

We were all bunched together for the check-in and luckily I was seated with Manoj. I knew my journey would be full of questions. "Ananya, I have conveyed it to the seniors there that you have a good grasp on the working of the company and how to raise the financial prospects of the company. So please try to mix up with the people there and don't be so cold and aloof. Otherwise, there would be a problem in cooperation and we have only three months' time."

This was the main reason why he had wanted to sit with me.

"I understand, Manoj, and I will try my level best."

I closed my eyes and thought about how I was not so cold and distant like this before. I used to be bubbly and chirpy. Rather, it was Sahil who was so cold and distant.

Sahil changed my life completely. It is so true, love can either make you or break you, and he had broken my heart into pieces and had turned me like this.

"Ananya, we are about to land. Just tie your seat-belt," shouted Manoj.

Ten minutes later, we were at the airport with our luggage. We were seated in a mini bus and proceeded to our destination.

I had come to Bangalore for the first time. It looked like a clean city, just like him. I imagined that he must be living somewhere there with his wife, enjoying his time. I had come to know through Karan that he had gotten married and was soon expecting his first child. That was the last I had talked to Karan.

How could he move on so easily? Was he just passing his time with me? Was his love just an illusion? I prayed secretly that I don't bump into him at any point of time for as long as I was staying there.

It was a big place with the main guest house located in the centre, surrounded by small cottage-like rooms. There was a lot of greenery everywhere, supported by many plants and trees alongside the guest house, making it a pleasant view to look at. We all were escorted by a guard from the guest house. The entrance gate was carved beautifully and there was a big hall inside. It was divided into two parts.

The wooden flooring was of dark-brown colour, in contrast with the off-white coloured walls. To the right, I could see an open kitchen near which there was a small dining table kept with six chairs. In the other corner, there was a big dining table with lots of chairs. There were no rooms downstairs. My eyes then caught sight of a staircase going up. It was also off-white in colour. I could see three rooms on the first floor, all of which had mahogany coloured doors matching the dining table. We were asked to sit and drinks were served. Soon after, we heard footsteps and looked towards where the noise came from.

In front of us stood a tall man in his mid-thirties with broad shoulders and a lean body. His eyebrows were thick and sharp and he had a strong jaw which was covered in a short stubble. He had a wheatish skin-tone, suiting him and making him look good.

Kavya could not take her eyes off of him, neither could the other girls.

Manoj stood up to greet him.

"Hi, Mr. Samar," he said and they shook hands.

"I hope you had no problem coming here," he said in his commanding voice, without a trace of a smile.

"Guys, he is the head of the finance department here and all the financial investment decisions are under him."

I looked at him worriedly. He seemed colder than even me. I wondered how I would work with him.

Cutting Manoj in between, Samar continued, "Let me introduce myself, Manoj."

"Yeah sure," Manoj turned pale under his stare.

"Welcome to my place. You all can live here in peace. Lunch, dinner and breakfast will be served here as the small cottages have no kitchen. I will make sure you guys will not face any problem, but there are certain rules in this house. One, nobody is allowed to enter the kitchen as the food will be served on the table. My family stays upstairs, so nobody will interfere in our life."

"Who all are there in your family?" asked an over-exited Kavya.

"Lastly, you all have come to work here. It's better if you maintained that relation without dragging my family into it. . We prefer our privacy. Enjoy your stay here. We will talk about business in our office tomorrow.

Manoj, I need to know who is the best in finance here."

Manoj looked towards me.

This man was so stern that I knew he wouldn't tolerate any mistakes. How would I cope with this monster, I wondered. I felt as if I was meeting people like Sahil everywhere; Ritvik who looked like Sahil, and this Samar who acted like Sahil.

We all moved towards the guesthouse. God Samar is so hot said one of the girls, but he is so cold.ya, maybe his wife is quite strict with him and they started giggling. These girls and their fantasies, I had thrown myself into work when I was their age.

Zoya and I were to stay in the same room and she was a bit nervous about that, I was happy that I'm not staying with Kavya or the other hr trainees who were beautiful cunning young girls.

Ma'am which bed you want, asked a nervous Zoya.

Zoya please don't be nervous and treat me like your friend and roommate here I said smiling

making her relax, and stop calling me ma'am, just call me Ananya ,don't make me look like old heartless woman.

Ok ma'am oh sorry aa Aanaya she stammered.

The trainees were sent together with us, so that the managers can put in their hard work along with the team. Ananya ma'am ,oh sorry Ananya lets go for dinner said a beautiful Zoya who had changed into her thin strap light pink colour night suit.

Zoya are you going to wear this there.

Ya Ananya, this is my night suit she said innocently.

Why is it not looking nice.

No you are looking beautiful?

I was still wearing my office suit and working on my laptop.Ok, give me 5 min and I quickly changed into my off white top and my jeans. Zoya looked towards me shocked may be because she saw me the first time in jeans ,or maybe she preferred me to wear a night suit, but she did not say anything.

When we reached the main house, everybody else was seated at the big table except Manoj, and to my chargrain, most of the girls had changed into pretty night suits,Whom they were showing off. I thought Zoya was not appropriately dressed, but when I saw other wearing kapris, sphagetii and shorts and Kavya was wearing a single knee length beautiful nighty showing her beautiful toned legs. Did they all went for shopping before comingI wonder

Everybody was staring me for my choice of clothes when we reached for the dinner, but I was feeling too awkward wearing my night suit and come out, as my night suit was like them ,but the fabric was cotton ,unlike silk and it was too simple, off white in colour ,with a Mickey mouse drawn on it.

Dinner was served, thin sambjar dal and idly and bada. I could see frowning faces, but I liked south Indian, not a problem for me.I could see no body on the dining table kept next to us, and then I saw Samar coming from up stairs, changing into a black track suit and navy blue colour t shirt a perfect sight for the girls as their eyes were glued at Samar. I was about to get up, but Zoya hold my hand; looking towards Samar, she said please sit for sometime.

I gave her a horrified look before smiling Zoya, what will Vikram say, I teased her.

Oh, forget about him right now and we laughed.

girls were standing slowly and trying to gain Samar's attention, but he was too engrossed in conversation with Manoj who got the privelage to sit with Samar

As I stood up to go, Manoj shouted my name too confidently.

ohh no, not now Manoj. I looked back to find both the man looking in my direction.

Can you please come here for a minute.

Yes Manoj, I can feel Samar's stare at me.

Please sit, he gestured me to sit in front of Samar.

Samar she is one of the best in finance, she had generated lots of profit to our company and is immensely talented. Ohh Manoj don't do this, don't increase his expectation I don't even know what I had to do here. He raised one of his eyebrow in an arch and said, well I hope you will be some use to the company. I looked toward him now with my sharp look, making him realize don't throw your attitude at me.This is why I have been brought here, I snapped at him.He stared at me for a minute and then said; ok, let's meet tomorrow in the office then.

Ya sure, I said with a straight face and stood up and went straight to the door ,without wishing both of them goodnight.

God,heissoarrogantandhowdareheunderestimated me.Okay, we are staying in his guest house for free, but still that snob had no right to behave like this.

I was fuming while going to my room, but when Ritvik's number flashed on the screen my smile return.

So you said you will call when you reach.

Oh, sorry Ritvik I got stuck up here.

So how are you?

I'm fine; I think you need to come here earlier.

Why are you missing me he teased?

No there is someone so arrogant who need your counselling.

who Samar he said at once.

Oh, you know him.

Yes, I know him very closely.

Is he your friend?

I will tell you once I come there not on the phone.

Wow, this is something strange.

So do you know his entire family?

Yes, I do personally, he is so cold, like you he quipped but he is a nice person, just a little harsh due to his problems.He is more concerned about his work than anything else, and I know he will be soon impressed with your work, but you need to be careful with his younger brother ,just stay out of his reach.

He has a brother also.

Yeah, and he is colder then Samar and he freak out a lot if anybody comes in his way,

Ok, so the whole family is like this.

Ritvik smiled, senced pain in his voice.

"Ritvik are you ok ,what happened?"

I'm fine Ananya, once I'm there I will let you know everything, they all are good people, but certain problems had made them people like this, I wish I could had helped them out with my calibre but I'm restrained to do and now you take some rest, I will call you later and he disconnected the phone.

What was wrong with Ritvik, he never behaved like this before. He was reluctant to tell much, but still he told me a lot, I need to be careful dealing with Samar.

Zoya was talking with Vikram on her phone, seeing me she brought her phone down guiltly.

"Zoya it's ok, you can talk, and I'm off to sleep."

"Thanks Ananya," she said.

Chapter 15

I woke up early in the morning and saw Zoya sleeping a peaceful sleep. How lucky she was, not having any work pressure while I would be burdened with lots of work with that arrogant Samar. I wore my best pair of trousers and white shirt and my flats as I was comfortable in it, I was first to reach the office followed by the others.

Kavya entered in her high heels and tight low waist trousers, crisp white shirt and lots of make up on. She was looking pathetic to me. I remembered how Sahil had scolded me once when I had worn makeup. "Anu, you are a natural beauty, don't mess up your beautiful face with these fake things," and I don't remember when I had put make up after that.

"Everybody please move inside the inner cabin where Samar will join us in 5 minutes," said Manoj holding some papers in his hand and bringing me out of my Sahil zone.

"Ananya, can I have a word with you?"

Crap! I was done for. Manoj was giving me his same lecturing look.

"Ananya what's wrong with you?"

"What have I done now?"

"Don't be innocent. Look at the way you talked to Samar yesterday and did not even wish him good night; he is your manager!"

"So what Manoj? You never talked to me like this, he is so arrogant."

"Ananya please, you will be reporting to him and he will provide the feed back in our company. Please don't mess up with him, for your sake. Had you talked to Ritvik?"

"What is he to do in this?"

"I wall ask him to call you."

"Manoj please don't drag him into all this."

"He needs to be dragged in this, as only he can make you understand."

What the hell!

"Let's go, Samar must be waiting."

When manoj and I entered the room which was occupied by a big round table and broad black chairs. Samar was standing and explaining something on the board, he looked towards me and then faced the other side. Wow that's nice! I gave Manoj a cold look and he gestured to me to sit. I could see only those people who were involved in the finance department; thank god Kavya was not there." Guys I hope you all will support us to bring our company back to normal," said Samar after explaining the facts and figures. "Mr Deepak is waiting outside for you all and he will assign you places.

Miss Ananya can we discuss the details?" Said Samar in his cold voice,

"Yes, sure sir, I'm looking forward."

"Ananya the finance department has undergone a great loss in the past few months and it is this department we need to bring back alive. All the minute details are mentioned in this file, go through them and we can sit together and discuss them tomorrow. The person who is looking after the investment will be coming back tomorrow, as you don't know much about the company, he will be of great help to you."

"And he is Samar's younger brother, brilliant like you," said Manoj, regretting later.

Samar stared at Manoj who became quiet, "He is not my brother here Manoj but only my employee."

Oh! the man Ritvik asked me to stay miles apart from. I would need to work with him.

The whole day went in a jiffy reading the godforsaken report; the company really needs hard work.

I was too tired to go for dinner in that big house full of morons, but Zoya dragged me, "Ananya, you are working so hard, you need to eat." I did not even bothered to change my office clothes as I was too tired to do that. Kavya gave me a disapproving look, but I really didn't care. My head was spinning like a cart wheel. One of the interns commented saying Ananya ma'am is so tired on the first day, how she will manage and they giggled and she is still wearing her office dress. Someone else added, "She is so lucky to be sitting with Samar and I had heard that his younger brother is joining from tomorrow and he is hotter then Samar and he is a divorcee."

Wow lovely family, I thought. After having that sambhar and dosa I went off to my room.

Next day I reached office along with the file which I had studied all night and had jotted down all the points to discuss; there were so many loopholes which were neglected.

What these brilliant brothers were doing in the company I had no idea.

The peon directed me to the conference room, where Kavya and Natasha were sitting. Natasha was from the HR department. Samar came inside and stood in front of us and addressed us saying, "Guys we need to work hard together to save this company, whether it is operation HR or the finance people," he looked towards me. "There will be one more person joining us today who will explain the working of the company in detail." Kavya's eyes were fixed at the door. The door opened and a tall man walked past us and stood there near the table with his back towards us, talking to Samar and Manoj. He turned and my body froze as if I had suffered a sudden paralysis. My heart rate increased tremendously and I shivered in disbelief, getting the most dreadful shock of my life. Intentionally I threw my file down and in an attempt to pick up, I quickly turned and made my way to the door.

"Ananya!" Manoj called out to me but I could not stop. I ran straight to the washroom, splashing my face with cold water. I still couldn't believe I saw him standing there.

My Sahil, no, not mine anymore. Sahil is Samar's brother that's why they had certain similarities. Oh god what do I do? Where the hell do I go now? Why did I have to confront him again after such a long time? I need to work along with him…No way! What do I do now? He left me 5 years back and now I should not bother whether he is here or not, I tried to pacify myself.

Zoya came rushing and asked if I was okay. I had got her worried too.

"Ya I'm fine Zoya," lets go back I said collecting myself.

"Did they say anything Zoya?"

"Ya, Samar said what nonsense is this, and the new manager...

Zoya flushed, "He said, I want this girl out of my team."

What the hell, I felt bouts of anger for crying for him right now.

"Let that man say this to me on my face. Let's go Zoya." I opened the door and everybody looked towards me owing an explanation. Now it was his turn, he froze in his chair with his mouth open in shock. I stared at him in his eyes; it looked as if he was paralyzed, good.

"I'm sorry Samar. I was not feeling well." He turned his face the other side. Wow, so like his younger brother.

"Manoj we will not tolerate this girl in our team who does not respect her seniors."

I saw Kavya and Natasha giggling. "Mr. Samar, I was not feeling well, was it ok with you if I would have vomited all the dirty sambhar which I ate in the morning on the entire table?"

Samar looked towards me wide eyed and Manoj slapped his forehead with disgust.

Samar was about to say something but his younger brother came out of his paralysis,

"Miss Ananya don't waste time and please take your seat. I hope you are feeling better now."

I ignored him and sat down; I could see Samar looking with disbelief towards Sahil.

Sahil stood up explaining the things that need to be worked upon. But it was difficult for me to concentrate, he had changed, he had gained a little weight and looked more muscular, maybe he had started working out. But his behaviour was the same, cold, like he used to be in college before meeting me, but looks wise, he had improved and I look so bland in front of him. Natasha was gossiping that he is a divorcee. Good, I'm happy his wife left him, jerk. I had not payed attention to anything that was said. "This was all for today," said Sahil.

"So Miss Anaya," said Samar, "Are you ok with what Sahil discussed about the future investment?

Samar sensed my reluctance. I was quiet for the first time and answered nothing.

"Manoj this is the girl you were full of praises for? She had not even payed attention. She just knows how to answer back." Manoj bowed his head and was quiet like me.

"You are right bhai," said Sahil, "She is good for nothing. I don't think her basics are clear."

"Oh really Mr. Sahil," he must have forgotten how I use to help him out to clear his basic I thought to myself

That's it. I said, "I was not feeling well that's why I was not able to concentrate and Mr Sahil you need to worry about your basics first then point out to others."

"See Manoj this girl needs some help," and Samar stood up and walked out of the room. Manoj also stood up and said, "Ananya, you are impossible," and he also walked, leaving me and Sahil together.

I rose up to leave but was interrupted by Sahil, "Miss Ananya."

Without looking at him I said, "Go to hell, you cheater!" And closed the door on his face.

I felt much better now, but my tears did not stop flowing. How dare he, I'll show him how clear my basics are and he will regret. He left me and now he is behaving like the most arrogant man, he must have never loved me, I'm sure about it now and I hate him all the more. I controlled myself and forgetting read the points which I had made, I cannot mess up with Samar, so I stood up and went to his cabin. He was sitting with Manoj and he looked the other way in disgust when he saw me. He did not ask me to sit.

"Sir, I just came to apologize for my behaviour", it was now he was looking toward me, "but seriously, I was not well, that's why I was not able to pay attention. Please let me explain my points which I had found lacking in this company and then you can take your decision of throwing me out."

He looked at me warily of what I was saying and then he asked me to sit. A while later Sahil also joined us. I rose and walked towards the board and made them go through the loopholes one by one, making them listen attentively. I saw Manoj smiling with pride. "That's all from me for today."

"Ananya I'm impressed," said Samar, "And the loopholes which you mentioned, we neglected those. Let's forget the past and work on the future and help us to retrieve our company."

"Right sir, it's of no use dwelling on the past," I said, looking towards Sahil, who was quiet and listening. He stood up at once and said he needed to prepare for a meeting.

Good, now you see how clear my basics are looser I grinned back at him

Ritvik was asking me to stay away from him. He does not know that Sahil will never mess with me, if he had little bit of shame.

Later at my room I changed myself into a flowing top paired with jeans and along with Zoya went to get my dinner.

Natasha was wearing a sexy night dress, whom these girls want to impress, there was a competition I guess between Kavya and Natasha. "Yaar when will he come?" Natasha said, looking up the stairs. "Who Samar?" asked Kavya arching her brow.

"No, I'm talking about Sahil."

"Stay away from Sahil, ok?" said Kavya grinning. "Natasha he is not of your type."

"Kavya and you are his type." In order to be cool with Natasha she said, "Ananya is his type" and I choked with my food which for a change was not south Indian today, and everybody started laughing.

"Nice joke Kavya," I said gulping, my food down.

Today the whole family came together for dinner except Sahil. "Where was he? I hoped he will come to take his dinner. I want to see him yaar," said Natasha impatiently. Girls were still crazy for him.

"He will come when the dinner will be half finished and leave before us," I quipped eating my food. They gave me a disgusted look and laughed. When we were in the middle of our meal; Sahil came rushing down the stairs, leaving the girls, gasping at him. I smiled to myself you were laughing at me na, now Kavya you will not be able to sleep, bitch.

Sahil finished his dinner before us and left.

Natasha stood up and asked me how I knew this.

"Kavya said that I'm his type, that's why I know," and then Zoya and I laughed out loud.

"But how did you know this?" Asked a Zoya confused while we were returning to our room.

"I only guessed it."

She raised her eyebrows in appreciation. I don't think she has still got it.

Chapter 16

Next day morning when I was entering the big house for breakfast, Sahil was coming out and we came face to face with each other more closely this time. He looked towards me and then turned his face the other side and walked past.

I couldn't stop myself from quipping, "Don't do this again with me. It should be me who needs to turn my face the other side."

Sahil turned and came towards me and said, "Then you do it the next time.

"I'm not a looser like you." I said and walked away without listening if he had to say something.

Mr. Sahil, now I will torture you every day. Just wait and watch, I thought to myself. I quickly grabbed my breakfast and went to office as I had a meeting with all of them again. So, I had prepared all of my reports properly. When I went inside, Samar politely said, "Please come Ananya." Ritvik was right. Samar was impressed with my work and he was not commenting any more. I probably should ask Ritvik how I should deal with Sahil, but no, I can deal with him on my own.

Sahil was engrossed in his paperwork,.

"Ananya, Manoj and I are leaving to brief the other department. I will like you to discuss the report with Sahil," Said Samar, standing up from his chair.

Oh shit, alone with him! I started sweating just thinking of being alone with him.

Sahil saw me and gave me his ghost smile for the first time, and I knew he knows I'm scared. I was lost in his smile for a second; going blank.

"Ananya, is it all right?" asked Manoj seeing me nervous."We will be back in an hour."

Crap! One hour alone!?

Ananya, you can do this. You are a brave girl, I said to myself and thought ok, just show him that you are not affected by his presence. I sat in front of him and said, "These are the conclusions I have arrived at. You can go through it."

He took the paper from me and said, "I will go through them later. I'm doing something important right now.

"Excuse me", I blurted. "I'm not a fool to keep waiting for you; your brother had asked me to discuss it with you."

He glared at me.

"I'm not afraid of your stare, okay?".

"Ok, fine." He snapped and said, "Tell me what is written".

"You have it in front of you."

He ran a finger on his left brow to calm his throbbing vein. "Ananya stop irritating me, I have a hell lot of work to do."

I snatched the report from his hands and said, "I will complain to Samar that your brother is not interested. He looked towards me bemused and said, "When will you grow up you? You are such a baby."

I remembered how he used to tease me for being a baby.

I couldn't help but snap, "And you had grown up into the arrogant old man who is recently divorced." He was aghast. He looked towards me wide eyed.

"You are a looser. And don't you dare call me a baby again." I was about to leave when Samar entered the room and accidently blocked my way. "Sorry guys, I just forgot my phone. Hey Ananya, are you both done so soon?"

"No Samar, he is too busy to study my report." Samar fumed with anger. Although he didn't utter a word but it was visible. Sahil stood up and said, "Sir, I was preparing for.." Samar interrupted him in-between and said, "This is the most important thing at the moment and Mr. Sahil, you are very well aware about our company's situation."

"Sorry sir", said Sahil and for the fraction that his eyes met mine, I gave him my smile this time.

Samar turned towards me and said, "Ananya, you can use Sahil's cabin till you are done."

We both were shocked and this time Sahil address him as – "Bhai please, I can't tolerate her in my cabin." I added, "Even I don't want to sit with him."

"What is the problem between you two?" asked Samar. "If you both will not cooperate, how will you work as a team?" And he left us with no choise.

Sahil picked up his laptop and said, "Come after me".

"Sahil I'm not your employee. Ask me to walk along with you," I snapped.

"Ananya, you have become so frustrating. Okay, walk along with me, ma'am."

"Thank you. You made me like this." I said with a straight face that made him shake his head in disgust.

All eyes were on us when we walked alongside. Natasha and Kavya must have died seeing this, I was smiling to myself. Sahil's cabin was quite big in comparison to mine. There was a big black table, clean, without any things cluttering it, unlike mine and on the right corner a small calendar was placed. It made me remember about Ritvik's table which was also clean like this. "You can sit there", he pointed towards the right corner where one chair was placed.

"What the hell! I'm not going to sit in that corner. I'm not your peon!"

"Okay, so you can sit anywhere you like," and he quickly went and sat on his chair.

I decided to sit with him at his table. I placed my purse on the right side of the table and a note pad to my left and my phone in front of my lappy, occupying almost half of the table. I knew he will not like it. He wanted to say something, but he somehow managed to be quiet. We both were busy preparing for our reports talking to each other only for any query. Ram knocked and came inside with a tray of food, for Sahil.

It was lunch time; I looked at the clock which was displaying 2PM. We had been really engrossed in our work. "Bring one more plate for m'aam," said Sahil to Ram.

"No, thanks. I'm going to the canteen. I need some fresh air," and I stood up and before moving out of the door, turned around and said, "I will be back in an hour."

"The lunch break is only 1 hour long, Miss Ananya. Please remember." he said with a scoff.

"I know," and I was on my heels heading out of the door, smiling.

Zoya saw me in the canteen and shouted, "Ananya! join us". She was sitting with the Delhi staff.

"Ananya, you seem to be very busy with Sahil," Commented Natasha.

"Natasha, I'm not busy with him, but with my work." Kavya was enough for me and now this Natasha also started. We all knew she was crazy for Sahil. I went back exactly in an hour but Sahil just ignored me. I was feeling so sleepy post lunch that for a moment I bowed my head on his desk to get some shut eye.

He did not say anything for some time. But that was only for some time.

"Miss Ananya, the senior managers are always taking rounds at this time, so please start working."

"I'm feeling sleepy."

"This is not your house Ananya," he said with a higher pitch and I knew it was better to sit up.

I opened my lappy when Manoj came inside.

Sahil gave me his all professional look.

"How is the report shaping up?" Manoj asked.

"Good, sir", said Sahil.

Manoj then turned to me and queried, "Ananya, I hope you are comfortable here."

I smiled and said, "Yes sir, I'm ok. Happy within a good company."

Manoj smiled and looked towards Sahil who was clearly looking unhappy. "Manoj, we will submit the report by evening." said Sahil cutting off his futile conversation.

"What! Have you gone out of your mind!?" I shouted at Sahil, making Manoj jump too. "So much work is left. I need tomorrow's time." By this time Samar had also joined us.

He added, "Its ok, I can grant you one more day but there should be no mistakes at all.

"Sir, we have 4 hours. We can complete it today." insisted Sahil.

I could not control myself and blurted angrily , "Sahil I'm not a horse. Okay? My eyes are hurting working on the laptop for so many hours." I could see disbelief on Samar's face as he must have not seen anybody talking to Sahil like this.

"Ananya, you had taken a break during lunch, I'm the one who's working continuously." Sahil continued the argument.

"Mr. Sahil," I got all professional and serious, "If you want to stay glued onto your seat like a bee, it's not my fault.You can also take a break."

Manoj signalled me to be quiet but when I glanced at Samar nervously, he was smiling.Thank God!

He came to my rescue. "Ananya, I totally agree with you. Sahil, you need to take a break. Go and grab a coffee. You look tired."

"Bhai please, I'm okay. Just ignore Miss Ananya. She can distract anybody."

"Oh, I'm shocked my brother got distracted for the first time." Said Samar smiling.

"It's good to see you two have gelled up together."

"Sorry, we can't gel up together ever," I muttered softly..

"Whatever...Now I'm leaving you guys to take a break and then you both can continue working. I know all thjis hard work has been tough on you." Even Samar wanted his brother to ease out a bit, but thankfully Samar's attitude had changed towards me. These brothers show that they are tough from outside, but they carry a gentle heart within.

"I'm going to have a coffee. You want me to bring one for you? I turned to see a brooding Sahil asking me that question.

No, thank you. I hate leaving things in between. But of course, you like leaving people without any reason." I retaliated with pain, and for a minute I saw him pained too. Guilt was written all over his remorseful and regretful face, but then I was confident this was plainly a facade. He said nothing, just kept looking at me with his big eyes but did not move.

I quickly stepped out of his cabin but I could not control myself and tears came trickling down my eyes.

I wiped them quickly before anybody could see. Reached the coffee machine and quickly made 2 cups of coffee. I knew he was very tired from working continuously.

"Oh, you have started making coffee for him as well", said Natasha grinning.

"Yes, do you have any problem?"

"Ananya, this is your real position, making coffee for people. Look at yourself, you look dreadful and that trouser and shirt you are wearing looks pathetic as your face. A boy like Sahil will never be interested in you. I don't know how he is tolerating you in his cabin." She venomed.

"And do you think he will tolerate a woman like you, who is cake faced in his cabin? I put particular stress on HIS cabin.

"I told Kavya and I'm telling you as well stay away from him."

"God! Natasha you are too much. Please let me go now and he is all yours if you are asking about my interest in him. I quickly took my coffee cups and marched out of her reach." Goodness! Everyone is after this arrogant boy, I muttered to myself and then looked down at my clothes. Natasha was right. I did need to work upon my looks now. I went inside the cabin and placed his coffee in front of him.

He looked up and said, "I did not ask you to bring me coffee."

"But you need it, right? And tomorrow you will bring coffee for me."

"What!?"

"It's obvious.. isn't it?"

He ignored that, took his cup and started taking small sips.

"Thank you," He said.

"I don't need your thanks. I need coffee tomorrow."

He shook his head in exasperation and said a louder than needed, "Okay".

By six I was ready to leave closing my lappy.

"If you want, you can come along with me. I'm also going home." Offered Sahil closing his lappy.

"No thanks and don't ask me again." I did not want him to feel that I was still crazy for him.

Plus, I had fixed an autowala for my to and fro to office and he was waiting for me and Zoya outside the building.

"Ma'am aaj jaldi free ho gaye."

"Yes," I said and Zoya gave me a naughty smile. To change where the conversation could have gone, I asked her, "Zoya, can you help me out in doing some shopping this weekend? "Shopping! Wow! I love going shopping!" She got all excited.

Once home, I quickly change into my jeans and top and we headed for dinner.

"Ananya, you are a senior manager and you don't have a night suit," commented the spiteful Natasha.

"I do, but I guess night suits are meant to be worn indoors." Natasha giggled like anything, making fun of me. "Ananya, you are so old fashioned. You should have been born in the 16 century."

I ignored her and we sat away from her, had our meal and returned to our room.

I finally changed into my night suit and lay down thinking about Sahil. He looked torn and depressed. I could make that out. I got thinking, and where was his controlling dad who ruined my life? Maybe he had been the one who forced Sahil to marry. But he could have told me, at least once. He went away leaving just a message.

I remembered how I had called him so many times and finally when he had picked up, "Hello Sahil!" I was dying to hear his voice.

"I'm Samar. Look Anu, he can't talk to you ever now. Please stop calling him."

"Bhaiya please," I pleaded. I had talked to Samar once before, wishing him on his birthday and he was happy talking to me.

"Anu, I know it's painful but, I can't help you guys any more on this," and he hung up. The world is so small and now he is in front of me. Thank God, Sahil had not told my full name to Samar bhaiya.Crap! Why was I addressing him as bhaiya?

Ritvik's phone call broke my chain of thoughts.

"Hi Ritvik."

"Ohh, so you are alive. I thought you got buried under your work."

"Very funny, Ritvik."

"Ananya, what happened? You sound low. I hope Samar is not giving you a tough time.

"Oh, not him but his brother Sahil is giving me one."

"What!? Sahil!!" He shrieked.

"Yes, we are working together on the same project."

"When did he join Samar?"

"That I don't know."

"Ananya, Sahil is good at insulting people and if he crosses his limit ever, just let me know." "Ritvik relax, I can handle him.You don't need to worry."

"I am sure of that, Ananya."

"What is with him? You have nay idea of what's his life like?" I asked trying to know something…anything more about him.

"Oh, he is a divorcee. He was forced to marry a girl of his father's choice but it did not work out, as he was in love with some other girl."

In love with some girl. The sentence reverberated in my head and my heart sank.

"Ananya are you ok? Don't think much of him. He is depressed, so he takes out his anger on others but I know you can handle him. Just don't push him too hard or he is known to explode and it becomes difficult to control him then.

"Ritvik how come you know so much about him? Are you guys friends?"

"Ananya I will tell you the details when we meet."

"Why not know?"

"Because certain things are complicated and need explanation face to face."

"Okay counsellor, how is Priya?"

"Oh, she is good. We met yesterday and you have no idea how she missed me!"

"Really wow! That's great. Let's hope she drops the idea of going to the US. I will pray for you, Ritvik."

"Its okay Ananya." He said solemnly. "If she will not agree, then you are there. I can marry you and I will even help you out in the kitchen for sure." And we both laughed out hard.

After Sahil it was Ritvik who knew how to make my sour mood good. In such a little time we had become good friends but how could he be related to Sahil and how will Ritvik react when he knows that Sahil was my Ex-boyfriend?

I recalled what he had said about Sahil being a divorcee now because he loved some other girl and my tears wouldn't stop flowing. So, he *was* forced to marry that girl but why did he did not say anything? Was he so weak? I had cursed him every minute of these 5 years, and look I was successful. My curse had shown its effect. He is so unhappy. I could see it on his face, but I was hurt and angry for not trusting me and confiding in me. Zoya saw me crying and asked if I was okay.

"Mood swings, Zoya. You know how we are when we have our periods."

"If you want something, Ananya, do let me know." She said helpfully.

"Ya sure, Zoya. Thank you," I smiled but I had started to feel the pain in my lower abdomin and I knew slowly it will become unbearable, just as I was used to it now. So I quickly took out a pain killer and popped it in my mouth and tried to sleep. But thoughts of Sahil were haunting me now, after I knew that he was forced into marriage. Yet it was not easy to forgive him. I closed my eyes and remembered how Sahil had panicked when he saw me in pain, "What happened, Anu? Should I take you to a doctor," he had said clasping my hand. Niya had laughed and said, "Buddhu, she doesn't need a doctor. These cramps are normal in these days."

"What days?" he had asked, mystified.

"Anu, I did not know your boyfriend was so dumb." Said Niya and I giggled even through the pain.

Karan took him aside and explained. He came back a little embarrassed and so was I as I was not able to hide my pain. He became really cautious later, used to feed me with his hands and occasionally give me hot water to soothe the cramps. He cared so much that I used to forget those tortureous cramps every month.

Chapter 17

I woke up with a jolt accompanied by pain and knew that I was late. It was 8 in the morning and I was supposed to reach office early.

"Ananya, don't worry," said Zoya who was ready to leave. "I brought your breakfast to the room. You were not well that's why I did not wake you up." Zoya was such a sweetheart.

"Thanks, Zoya. Did anybody see you bringing the breakfast?" I asked and quickly started to get ready forgetting about my damn pain.

"Yes," Zoya blushed "Sahil, he asked me where am I taking the food and I told him you were not feeling well." Crap! Now he will know and this pain is not stopping. I quickly popped another pain killer and Zoya eyed me with disapproval.

"Ananya, you have not eaten anything," She said concerned.

"I will eat in the auto, Zoya, I'm already late." I reached the office and I knew I was looking a disaster;

with my shirt out of my trousers and my hair badly combed. I went inside Sahil's cabin without knocking and thank God he was not there, but his lappy was kept opened. I guessed he must have gone somewhere. I kept my bag and bowed my head over the table. I was tired of the pain and the crying. I woke up with the phone ringing and saw Sahil sitting in front of me.

Shit! I had slept and he was looking at me worried. He got up, unlatched the door and went outside. When the door clicked close, I took out a comb from my bag and slightly brushed my hair. Why is this pain not going? My stomach was rumbling with hunger too. Damn! I had forgotten my breakfast on the table. Sahil came back and placed a plate of sandwich and a cup of coffee in front of me.

"I don't need this, and why did you put the latch on."

"You were not well and sleeping and I did not want the seniors to see you snoring on my table."

"I don't snore," I said pushing the plate away

"See, you asked me to bring coffee, remember?" He said pushing the plate back towards me.

I didn't want to argue as I knew if I will not eat anything I will not be able to work. So I quickly ate my sandwich and drank my coffee.

"What time do we need to present our report?" I wanted to know.

"On Monday, so now you can relax." He replied.

"Why Monday?" I was surprised.

"Because our CEO had to go out urgently somewhere." He filled me in.

"Oh, thank God," I mouthed.

"But we have a group meeting after lunch," said Sahil, eyeing me carefully. "Have you taken your medicine?" He asked, worried.

I just gave him a stern look.

"I'm just asking."

I was feeling better now, so I started working on my report without replying to him.

Sahil stood up and again went outside and brought me a glass of hot water.

"Drink this." He ordered.

"I don't need your concern, Sahil. I'm not your girlfriend now."

He gave me his beautiful smile to melt me on purpose.

"I know, Ananya. I'm just giving you hot water."

"I don't want."

"So you will not drink it?" His tone was alarming.

"No, I won't," I was adamant too.

He took the glass. Came close to me, making me shiver and held my face and placed the glass near my mouth.

"I'm not moving until you drink this." He commanded.

I took 2 sips of that hot water and saw Samar coming inside. Samar froze seeing Sahil making me drink water like that. Nervous Sahil removed the glass in a jiffy and the hot water fell on my lap. "Ouch!" I grimaced. The water was really hot. I don't know how was I drinking it.

Sahil panicked, "Oh shit!" and brought a glass of cold water from the table and poured on me so that I get a little relief and in being quick he spilled the water on my shirt and my entire trousers.

"What the hell, Sahil!!" I shouted, standing up drenched in water.

"I'm so sorry, Ananya".

Samar was standing still like a statue and my shirt was clinging to my body.

"Are you ok, Ananya?" asked Samar in shock?

'No, I'm not. Your stupid brother has soaked me in water when I'm not feeling well.' I wanted to say this but somehow, I didn't. "I'm fine, Samar sir," was all I said.

Sahil was looking here and there as if he had committed a crime, finally he got some courage and he said, "Bhai, can you please leave us alone for a minute?"

"Yeah, sure bhai. Take care of her," and I know Samar was teasing Sahil now.

Once Samar went outside, I started crying like a baby. Whether it was the mood swing or because I was soaked, I don't know what triggered it but my tears wouldn't stop.

"Ananya, please don't cry. I can take you home and you can change your clothes."

"I don't want to go with you."

"And I'm not letting you go alone in this condition. You get that?" he asked in his harsh tone?

"How will I go out all soaked up like this?" I asked, more to myself than him.

"Take this. Wear my coat?"

"Oh no! It is so embarrassing."

"It's not!" And he placed his coat over my shoulders and picked up his car keys, and gently pushed my shoulder to indicate to move on.

"Please remove your hand; you wanted me to be killed

"What!?" He said in disgust.

"Your fans will see me with you and they have already given me warnings to stay away from you." I told him.

He smiled after a long time. "Do I have fans here? Wow! Who are they?"

"I'm not telling you the names," I replied.

"Ananya, I'm least interested in any woman." The serious Sahil had returned.

Thank God, it was lunch time and there was no staff in the office as they must have gone to the canteen. We reached the parking and I climbed in his car without noticing what kind was it.

"I'm sorry, Ananya," he said on the way, looking at me. "I had to explain a great deal to bhai." He said, looking sullen.

"What was the need to make me drink water with your hand?"

"Because you were being so stubborn!"

"Don't shout at me, Sahil," I shouted and was about to cry again.

"Ok, I'm not saying anything now."

He parked his car in front of my house and I quickly opened the door and moved out, so that I may not have to ask him in. I opened the padlock and felt Sahil behind me.

"What?" I asked him.

"Ananya, you want me to sit in the car till you change and come back? It's terribly hot." He reasoned.

"As if you don't have an AC in your car. You can go to your home. It's right there," I said, trying to not open the door, but he pushed the door and came inside saying, "Show some gratitude to the person who brought you here."

"Yes, the one who first threw hot and then cold water at me. Where will I change if you stay in the room?"

"Don't you have a washroom? And where do you sleep?" He sat on the bed and asked me.

"Mind your own business." I snapped.

I quickly opened my cupboard and took out my clothes. He kept looking at me.

"Stop staring, okay? And look at that side. I need to take out my clothes," I said.

"I'm not snatching your clothes, Ananya."

"Sahil, please I need to take out other thing as well."

"Oh, yes. Okay." He said, and turned the other way.

I grabbed hold of all the things and went to the bathroom and changed into my perfect fitting low waist trousers and short white shirt, which I usually wear to give important presentations and which was the best official dress I had. Sahil gave me his gawky stare but then quickly faced the other side. I brushed my hair to decency and applied some lip balm.

"Let's go." He did not hear me. He was just staring. "Sahil, let's go." I said a little louder. "Are you not going to wear your sandals?"

Oh shit! All my shoes were kept in Zoya's cupboard and it was locked and my flats were seeping with water. I decided I will have to wear Zoya's heels, which were lying outside. I took them out and tried them and they fit me perfectly.

"You are going to wear heels?" asked Sahil.

"I don't have any other option."

"Your back will pain more. As it is you are not well."

"I'm absolutely well, Mr. Sahil. Now let's go we need to attend the meeting."

Once there, I opened the door to the conference room and everybody was there waiting for us. Samar stood up and said, "Let's begin now".

Everybody was shocked to see me looking taller and smarter in my fitted low waist trouser. I knew they were jealous like hell, as Sahil walked behind me. I sat near Zoya and Sahil moved further and sat across the table in front of me.

"Manoj will brief you all with the latest update regarding the project," Said Samar.

"Ananya, you are looking hot," whispered Zoya.

"Sorry, I'm wearing your heels. I will tell you everything later."

"That's ok. You look so sexy!"

I could feel Sahil's eyes on me. Samar was standing in a corner listening to Manoj and then abruptly he looked towards Sahil. When I matched his glare, Sahil was looking at me, without blinking.

'Oh no! Sahil, stop staring. Samar is watching.' I somehow tried to convey through telepathy but he did not look the other way. Finally, the scheduled was over and everybody started to leave.

"Ananya and Sahil, stay," Said Samar, anger laden. "Manoj please wait for me in my cabin. I will be back in a minute." We both turned pale under Samar's pernicious stare.

"So Sahil, what did Manoj discuss here?" Questioned Samar. Sahil was dry-mouthed and could not answer. His face looked pale. Samar then faced me and asked, "Ananya, what did Manoj discuss here?" I bowed my head. "What the hell is wrong with you guys? What is going on?" He shouted. "My two most brilliant employees don't know anything that was discussed here in the meeting!"

"Sahil you need to thank God for me being smooth on you despite your carelessness." He pressed a button and Ram came running in. Ram keep an extra table and chair in my room, Miss Ananya will be sitting in my cabin from today, as I am mostly out in meetings." Sahil and I looked at each other as if we had committed a sin.

Samar stood up and said, "Whatever is going on between you guys, please sort it out before others get to know it and make an issue about it," And he left.

"Damn Sahil!" I shouted, "Why the hell were you staring!? Samar's eyes were just on you."

"I'm sorry, Ananya. You were looking so good."

"Please Sahil, stop this nonsense. There is no place left for all this shit now."

"I know," he hissed and rose slowly and left.

It was a bad day. I shifted all my things to Samar's cabin but then why I was feeling depressed? I needed to be happy that I'm not sitting in Sahil's cabin anymore but I was feeling terrible. The aches all over my body, the tiredness, the exhaustion and these stupid heels were making me crazy. I used to wear heels a lot at one point of time but now I was not used to these at all.

In the evening Zoya and I were waiting for our auto for the past 15 minutes.

"Zoya, how do you wear such high heels?" I asked, looking around for a place to sit but there was none.

"Let's search for another auto Ananya. I don't think ours will come today."

"Yeah, right," I said. We were about to cross the road when Sahil parked his car in front of us and offered us a lift.

Zoya blushed like a teenager. "No," I said, "We can search for an auto."

"Ananya, you will not get any auto now. All must be booked.

"We can come by bus then."

"Miss Ananya, please, I request you. I know you are not feeling well."

"Mr. Sahil, don't you understand I said no?" I fumed.

Sahil opened his car door and came and stood in front of me raging with anger. I also stared back at him. He opened the rear door and signalled Zoya to get in, which she did dutifully. He then held my hand firm and pushed me in the front seat and slammed the door shut.

"How dare you?" I smoldered.

"Zoya, do you have any problem sitting in my car?" He asked Zoya.

"No sir," Zoya stammered, "Not at all".

"Ananya, it's okay. It's just a 5 minute drive," Zoya cajoled me smiling.

Sahil came close to me. His face was inches away from me, making my heart beat faster. But he pulled the seat belt and snapped it and said, "Now it's ok," and started driving.

He stopped the car in front of my house. Zoya and I hopped out of the car. She said, "Thank you sir", but I did not say anything to him. "Bye Ananya," teased Sahil as the car moved and I knew he was enjoying. I remembered how Sahil and Karan used to tease me, calling me a baby.

I slept for the rest of the evening and only woke up to take my dinner as I was exhausted and famished too . As I was about to stand finishing my dinner I saw Samar coming towards me. "Ananya, I need to talk to you."

Ya sure sir and we moved to one of the sides.

'Oh no, this must be about Sahil,' and I remembered he had warned me to stay away from his family.

"Ananya see I'm not interfering between you and Sahil as you both are adults, but being Sahil's brother I can see that he is distracted a bit with you. Actually Sahil lost somebody whom he dearly loved and till date he has not forgotten that girl. He had cut himself from all the social gatherings, but today I saw him looking at you with admiration. Ananya, I should not ask you, but please tell me do you also have some feelings for Sahil?" I made a straight face and said, "No sir, but what made you think so?"

"Ananya, the way you were scolding him that day, and the way he was listening to you; I have not seen that in years, and that day when I saw him making you drink water from his hands, I thought that...I thought..." Samar was not able to complete his sentence.

My heart was crying now. Should I tell him that I'm the same girl? No I will not, otherwise they all will pester me to forgive him and I can't do that. He had made my life hell. I had cried so much for him.

"Ananya, I'm sorry if I crossed my line," Said Samar. "I just don't want to get my brother hurt again." Wow! Sahil has hurt me and Samar is worried about his brother. Incredible!

Samar's wife Ridhima had come there too by now. "Hey, Please come here for a minute." Ridhima looked beautiful with her fair skin and beautiful smile. Samar introduced me to her. "Meet Ananya." She gave me a warm smile and said, "Oh, so she is Ananya. Well, Ananya, I have heard a lot about you. Nice meeting you finally."

"Same here, Ma'am." I retorted..

Samar and Ridhima was about to leave when we saw Sahil's car coming. Samar whispered, "Ananya, please don't say anything to Sahil. He won't like it."

"Don't worry, sir, I understand."

Sahil came out of his car in anger and closed the door with a loud bang. He walked past us fuming with anger. I knew something terrible has happened. "Sahil, what happened?" Asked Ridhima, worried but he yelled at her saying, "Bhabhi, please. How many times have I told you not to interfere in my personal life?

"Sahil, I'm concerned.

"Bhabhi go and show your concern to Reem. She needs it more."

"Sahil is this the way to talk to your Bhabhi?" asked Samar stepping in between.

Sahil banged his hand on the table in fury which made the flower pot topple from the table and break into small pieces, collapsing on the floor. "What is wrong with this boy?" said an exasperated Ridhima and walked out in anger, making me and Samar stand like statues.

I could see pain in Samar's eyes but what was wrong with Reem? Where was she?

Samar came close to me and said, "See Ananya, this is the real Sahil I was referring to. His loneliness is driving him crazy and this is how he behaves now, shouting at the family members. Many a times I have talked to him that he needs to move on but I don't know how long will he lament for that girl; she, who must have got married till now and must be having her own kids.

Samar's statement shocked me as he did not know it was me.

"Anyway, I'm so sorry to bother you. I'll just go and check on Sahil," and he left me standing there absorbing in the shock. I had hated Sahil for a long time but my heart bled to see him in this pain.

Why did God do this with us!? I went back to my room crying. With a heavy heart, I layed down on my bed. Sahil used to love his family so much. What happened that he was talking to his bhabhi like this? Ridhima was so concerned, I could tell from her face. And what about Reem? Where was she? And Sahil had told me once that Samar and his wife were separating, so who was Ridhima? Zoya opened the door bringing me out of my reverie. She had so many bags with her it looked as if she had bought the whole place. "Ananya, what happened?" One look at me was enough to tell her I was upset.

I didn't want to spoil her mood, so I said, "Nothing Zoya, I'm fine. Just a bit tired."

"Is it about Sahil sir?" I could only nod. "Ananya, I don't know what you feel about Sahil sir but one thing is for sure that he really cares about you. I started to cry. I don't know why was it difficult to hold back my tears. "Hey!" Said Zoya holding both my hands, "I have never seen you so vulnerable. I want my Ananya ma'am back who used to scold us for small things."

I wiped my tears and said, "Thanks Zoya, but matters of the heart are just complicated sometimes."

She held my hands again and said, "Ananya you can share everything with me. I hope you know you can trust me." Trust—there was the word again.

"Zoya, all I can tell you is that we both know each other from a long time back, and because we were good friends it's sad to see him in so much pain. But a lot has changed since then between us."

"Why don't to talk to him? Maybe you can help him out."

"I want to, but I'm angry at him."

"Ananya, I don't think so you are as much angry with him as you are upset and pained to see him in pain, and if you are not able to see him in pain, it's a clear indication that you should help him out to come out of his situation, keeping aside your ego and hurt. And one more thing Ananya, have you ever tried to gauge from his point of view why you both are no longer friends?" Though Zoya was younger than me but still she understood me so well.

"Yeah, I need to find out first what's wrong." I affirmed.

Sahil was nowhere to be seen when I went for breakfast and then I saw him coming from the main door shaking dirt off his messy clothes. His dishevelled look spoke volumes that he was part of a brawl. Without waiting a second Kavya and Natasha ran towards him to save him from falling. "Creepy girls," said Zoya.

Sahil jerked his hand away from Kavya and said, "Just stay away."

"Sahil, what is wrong with you?" Asked a worried Samar. I was stuck to my chair horror bound. Sahil was drinking! I knew how he hated drinking and disliked people who would drink, because her father used to drink a lot.

Zoya kept her hand over my hand to make me calm down. Samar came forward, "Sahil, please stop creating a tamasha in front of everybody." "What?" He giggled like a baby. "Let everybody know how big a loser I'm. I'm a looser!" He shouted, making me guilty for calling him a loser too many times in the past. He again fisted his palm on one of the tables and the cutlery flew a few inches and came clanking down. I held my hand over my mouth. Why was he hurting himself again and again? Everybody was looking at him with horror.

Samar shouted looking at us, "Quickly finish your meals and please give us some privacy." Few people at once cleared the table as they were least bothered, but Kavya and Natasha did not move, neither did Zoya and I. Sahil slumped on the sofa and sobbed saying, "I'm a looser. I have lost everything."

In that moment a lady shouted in her shrill voice, "Samar!" She was tall and dusky, with sharp striking features, with a high pony which was accentuating her cheek bones making her features more sharp. She was dressed in an official attire; wearing a gray colour knee length skirt and a crisp white shirt along with a gray blazer matching her skirt which she teamed up with nude colour pumps. Her face was blazing with anger.

Seeing this Kavya and Natasha quickly stood up and moved. Ananya what are you waiting for? Get up," said Natasha looking at me. I was not able to reply. "We are coming in 5 minutes," said Zoya. Samar saw us, but did not ask me to leave. Possibly he saw something in my eyes. That lady came in shouting and threw the papers on Sahil's face in disgust as he laid there almost unconscious. "Samar, why can't your brother stay out of my life?" She shouted at the top of her voice. "How many times have I told him to stay away from my daughter?"

Sahil opened his eyes for a moment and said, "She is my daughter too." Oh no! Sahil has a daughter as well and the angry lady was his wife. "She is not your daughter. You are not her father, Sahil. Your interference is not letting her mix up with her real father."

Sahil stood up fumbling and said, "It was me who picked her up when she was born, it was me who bathe her for the first time, it was me who taught her to walk for the first time and now you are saying she is not my daughter. Where was her father when he left you pregnant and ran away?"

"He has apologised many times and I tried to work out my relation with you, but you were never interested. Please leave my daughter and me alone now. This is the legal notice that says you will not talk to my daughter anymore." She gritted.

Sahil slumped down on the sofa crying, Please don't do this to me."

"How can you send him a legal notice, Manyata? He has done so much for you and your baby," Samar fumed in anger.

"Samar, why don't you get him married so that he can have his own children or is he still brooding for that bitch who had made my life hell?"

"Manyata!" Shouted Sahil. "Don't bring her in between."

The girl they were talking about was standing in front of them but had I ruined Manyata's life or she mine and Sahil's.

"Your brother had become one frustrated drunkard that is why he is so alone." She continued. Her words were piercing my heart.

"Ananya, please we need some privacy," Said Ridhima. But I was unable to move. I wanted to slap Manyata hard on her face but Zoya dragged me outside. Samar looked at me confused as tears were welling down my cheeks too.

"Ananya please stop crying you will get sick." Zoya was caressing my back.

I could see that he was broken. He had always wanted love but what was all that Manyata was saying?

Chapter 18

My head was spinning hard in the morning when I woke up and so I took a disprin tablet and went to the washroom to get ready. I had to present the report today on which Sahil and I had been working for the past 2 days and I knew that Sahil would not be in the condition to come. I quickly got ready while sweet Zoya packed breakfast for me. "Was Sahil here?" I asked her She just shook her head. We reached office in time and I went to Samar's cabin, to where I had shifted recently.

Samar was engrossed in his paper work; thank God he did not look up or talk to me.

I took out my laptop and went through the presentation for the last time,

"Ananya are you ok? He asked, concerned.

"Yes, I'm fine. Actually I was working on the report and did not sleep properly maybe that's why I look a bit tired."

"Okay, as you know Sahil is not in a condition to come, so will you be able to pull it alone?"

"Sure sir, but when will he join?" I asked, worried.

"I really don't know. He is unwell." I could see his eyes were flooded with tears which he was trying hard to control. "He has not eaten anything from last night and he is not ready to listen to anybody."

"What!? He has not eaten anything since last night and you are telling me now." I knew I was louder than I should. Controlling myself I continued, "What I mean is that I could have tried to make him eat."

"Can you do this Ananya?" He asked hopefully.

"Yes, I will talk to him in the evening if that is ok with you."

"Yes, why not." Samar got over-whelmed and grasped my hand and said thanks. Was he the same arrogant man who had once asked me to stay away from his family?

He loves Sahil so much.

I gave the presentation successfully explaining all the details and our further plans to carry out our operations. "Well done, Miss Ananya, you had put in a lot of effort. I'm quite impressed," Said Mr Narayan, our CEO. "It's not alone my effort, sir," I said, "Sahil worked very hard with me. Unfortunately, he is not well today."

"Yeah, I know Sahil is immensely talented. He just needs to work on his interpersonal skills." Manoj smiled looking at me and I returned a small smile. It was time to leave office and I was a little scared to confront Sahil. Would he listen to me? What if he yells at me? Samar has such faith in me. Will I be able to help Sahil? No, I don't think he will yell at me. I will persuade him to eat no matter what he says. I will not let him ruin his health drinking alcohol. After changing my dress Zoya and I went for dinner. So you saw the full tamasha," commented Kavya who had started feeling lack of importance everywhere. Ignoring her I just kept looking at the staircase to have one glimpse of Sahil. Samar came down with Ridhima and without waiting for a second, I rose from my chair and went to Samar, making everybody looking at me in disbelief. "Hi, ma'am," I said to Ridhima. "What happened? Why are you both so upset? Where is Sahil? Has he eaten anything?" I asked all the questions I had.

"Ananya I don't know where he is and his phone is also switched off," Said Samar worried.

Before I could say anything, we saw an inebriated Sahil coming with a bottle in his hand.

"Oh no! He had been drinking again and that too first thing in the morning. Samar ran and clutched Sahil's hand. "Leave me alone!" He shouted. Ridhima did not move from her place, but she was clearly upset.

Once again I stayed glued to my place. People started moving out quickly finishing their dinner.

"Sahil, eat something," said Samar in a breaking voice. "Why are you punishing yourself? You have not eaten anything since last night."

"I don't want to eat," and he tried to make his way upstairs. I was not having pity on him this time and I really wanted to slap him hard for behaving like a jerk.

"You are not going anywhere," I said loud enough for everyone to hear. Ridhima and Samar look at me perplexed.

Sahil looked toward me and said, Now you don't start pestering me."

"I'm not pestering you rather I'm just telling you are not going anywhere without having your meals."

"I don't what to eat and you don't try to teach me. It's my house."

"Yes, I know it is. Now don't you force me to drag you to the dining table."

"Ananya just get lost," he snarled. This was too much for me now. I went close to him making him blink a 100 times, snatched the bottle from him and shattered it on the floor. The alcohol quickly flowed its way on the floor making the room stink.

Kavya and Natasha hurried to the door but Zoya stood near the door giving us privacy. "How dare you?" Said Sahil and before he could do anything I put my hand in his pockets and took out his phone and key.

He was unable to react because of the initial shock. "Ananya", he said aloud, "What the hell are you doing? Stop acting like a baby". "Sahil everybody knows who is acting like a baby here. If you are not able to handle your issues and so you come drinking and making others suffer with you, well, that makes you the baby. He was quiet for a moment, then said, "Since when have you been so selfish, just thinking about yourself? Give me my phone back., He said.

"Not unless you have your dinner."

"I don't want to eat."

"Sahil sir," A small stammering voice came from behind. Zoya was standing behind us.

He looked towards her waiting for her to say what she wanted to. "Zoya, no," I said. "Please leave. It's nobody's concern." I scolded her in my same harsh tone. I knew what she was going to say.

"Ok," She gave in but Sahil held her hand making all colour from her body drain. "What is it? Tell me," he insisted. Zoya looked at me. "I'm asking you to tell me Zoya."

"Ananya has also not eaten anything from last night,"

Zoya said. Sahil was in utter shock. He closed his eyes for a second. He then faced me and asked, "You had not been eating and you been working like a horse?"

"I will not eat until you eat and you know me more than anybody else." I replied.

Sahil shook his head in a fury and then held my hand and dragged me to the dining table and made me sit on the chair. I saw Samar relaxing and they all joined us on the table.

Ram served us in our plates. Sahil said to me, "Eat your food."

"Not before you," I quipped.

"You are so irritating," he made a face and started eating his food. Samar mouthed thank you and Ridhima gave me her warm smile with tearful eyes. After finishing Sahil said, "Give me my phone back." I kept my promise. "And I don't what to hear next time you are not eating," he said. "Same goes for you. It all depends on you." I calmly replied. Sahil gave me his exasperated look and went upstairs. "Ananya it's only you who can handle him. See, he is concerned about you not eating. I knew he felt something for you. Do you guys know each other from before?" Asked Ridhima sounding happy. "Yes, we were in the same class and I was his friend for some time. We got thick so I know him well enough to handle him, but that is all there is. Please don't contemplate anything more."

"But you had not eaten for him," Said Samar, confused. I smiled and lied, "I had asked Zoya to say this because I knew Sahil won't give in until he is made to feel guilty that because of him someone else is not eating." I was relaxed. Now they will believe there is nothing more to us. Smart move. Ridhima suddenly asked, "Do you know the girl he loved?"

"No," I said with a straight face. "She was in the other section. We did not have much interaction.

"Do you have a photo of hers?"

"No, all I know is that she is married now." I did not want them to run in search of me.

"Thanks," Said Samar.

"It's ok," I said and moved to the door hiding the tears streaming down my face.

Chapter 19

I reached office and went to Samar's cabin. Ram was cleaning the table; the only table. "Where is my desk?" I asked Ram and he told me that some foreign delegates are coming in so Samar sir has asked him to keep my things in Sahil's cabin.

Oh, I knew Samar did this for his brother's love, but it's ok I was more comfortable in Sahil's cabin than his. I went to Sahil's cabin and opened the door to see him working on his laptop.

He looked up but did not say anything. "Glad you are back to work," I said smiling.

"I thought if I will not go to work, you will also say you won't either and sit at home."

"Oh, that was funny Mr. Sahil."

"When did you go shopping?" He asked looking towards my new clothes.

"When you were wailing in front of your wife." God! I am rude.

He gave me a stern look and said, "My ex-wife. Were you there then?"

"Yes, I'm the prime witness that your ex-wife was accusing me of ruining her life." There was a frown on Sahil's face and I felt sorry to have taken him on that path again. I changed the topic and said, "I had presented the report yesterday as you were not there." I thought of asking about Reem, but it was for later. "So what did they say?" Asked Sahil narrowing his eyes. "They all were quite impressed and now we need to sit with the finance, HR and operations team and discuss the strategies with them," I filled him in with the details.

After going through the reports we all were gathered in the meeting room. Samar made the start, "So Miss. Kavya, kindly brief us with the report you have made."

"Yes, sure," Said Kavya, as she was dying to flaunt her curvaceous look wearing her tight clothes in front of Sahil. She took 15 minutes to explain everything while smiling and I can made out nobody was much impressed. "Miss Kavya and Miss Natasha you can discuss the details with Sahil and then frame a strategy to overcome the issues in the Operations and the HR department. The rest can leave and wait for their managers to be back," Concluded Samar.

No! Sahil would be alone with Kavya and Natasha, but why was I worried? It's part of his work and I knew Sahil will not tolerate their nonsense.

I was standing and watching Sahil engrossed in his files and Kavya and Natasha dying to be alone with him. "You can stay Ananya, if you want," said Samar seeing my reluctance to go and seeing me watching Sahil. Sahil looked up hearing this and said, "I don't need her now and I can discuss the financial plan later in my cabin." How dare he said, he doesn't need me now!

"Fine, I'm leaving and giving you the desired privacy which you are dying to have," I cooed sweetly and I could see Samar trying to curl his lips inside his mouth so that he could stop laughing.

"Ananya, you are wasting our time," Sahil wasn't pleased with what I said. I picked up the files and moved out with Samar giving Sahil I-will-teach-you-a-lesson-afterwards look. It was difficult for me to concentrate on my work. Why was he taking so long to discuss? I was pacing in Sahil's cabin churning out all the horrible thoughts in my mind.

"Can I come in?" asked Samar.

"Yes sir."

"Have you started working on the point which I made you write down?"

"...ahh no aa...Samar sir...I...umm...was about to start. Okay, I just need to add a few more points to it."

"Sit down. So, you said that we could cut down investment in the new projects and focus on our recent projects, but the projects which the company need to invest will give us, more profit, right?"

I was looking towards Samar, holding my pen. "Ananya!" He said bringing, me out of my distraction.

"Yes, sir. So what is it that you want to say?"

"I just told you." Samar smiled and asked, "What's wrong? Worried about Sahil?" And before I could say anything Sahil came inside grinning, ear to ear. "Hey bhai!" He said. "Sahil, how was your meeting?"

" It was very good bhai. Some girls are bestowed with beauty with brains."

I looked towards Sahil with utter disgust and said, "Why you don't ask that beauty with brains to join you in your cabin?"

"I wish I could, but my place is already occupied with..." He smirked looking at me.

"Samar sir asked me to sit here otherwise I have no intension to sit with a brooding bore old man like you."

Sahil laugh out hard making Samar look at his brother with surprise. He hadn't seen this Sahil in a long time.

"Who said, I'm old! Look at yourself, you are the one who looks old. You should learn how to dress up from Kavya and Natasha."

"Just stop it guys. Sahil no more jokes. And Ananya I will talk to you later as I'm calling a meeting in next 5 minute in my cabin," Said Samar leaving the cabin, smiling.

"I'm feeling so refreshed after meeting them," Said Sahil looking to gauge my reaction.

"From when did you start liking cake faced women?"

"Who was looking at their faces?" He said with a sigh. I opened my mouth in disgust but said nothing. I stood up and he asked, "Where are you going wearing that new dress?" I threw the papers which I was holding in my hands on the floor and yelled, "You do your work of fantasizing about those women."

"I'm least interested in these women," He said.

I gave him a disgruntled look and softly said, "Your office. Your mess. You can pick these papers up yourself." I knew he was grinning when I banged the door.

At the meeting, Samar said, "So guys I have called you all together because I have an announcement to make; we have organised a welcome party for you all. I know it's almost a month, but we did not get the time to announce the welcome party. Hope you guys come down for the party. The venue and time will be displayed on the board."

Natasha and Kavya were shouting like teenagers going out of the conference room.

"Sahil, I believe you won't be coming for the part, like last year," asked Samar while returning back to Sahil's cabin along with me.

"Bhai, you know I don't like these parties."

"Oh, really Sahil! What will Kavya and Natasha do without you?" I commented and Sahil gave me an arched look.

"I can take them privately somewhere without any interference. How about that?"

I pressed both my lips together in anger. Samar shook his head in a mocking smile. "Ohh God! You guys are too much. Go and do some research on the project which I gave you," and he went back to his cabin. "Ananya you will go wearing your trouser and shirt to the disc?" Asked Sahil laughing.

"Mr. Sahil, just wait and watch what I wear tonight."

"I would love to see you wearing nothing." My eyes were wide with horror, but I didn't know why I did not feel offended by his statement. If someone else would have said this, I would have thrashed him. But it was my Sahil and I could only say, "You are so sick," He laughed with all his heart. He still knew how to irritate me, but I liked that I was still able to bring him out of his sour mood. "Why are you not coming to the party?" I changed track.

"I have some reports to work upon, but if you face any problem there, just let Samar know and if he is not there just give me a call; the place is 10 mins away."

"I can take care of myself, Sahil."

"I know you can. Do you have my number?"

"No," I quipped, "I don't need your number."

He ignored and took out his phone and in a second, I heard a beep on my phone. "Save my number in case you need it."

Everybody was excited in the evening, but I was feeling jealous and annoyed.

How dare he call me old, today? There was a knock on the door, and I thought it must be Zoya, but I was shocked to see Samar standing in front of me. "Hi sir, please come in."

"No its ok. I just came to talk to you for a minute."

"Yes sir, tells me."

"Can I ask a favour from you?"

"Yes, why not? Can you convince Sahil to come to the party tonight. See he is not listening to me and I really want him to meet a very nice girl and I think she will be perfect for Sahil." I felt as if something pierced my heart deep.

"Are you okay, Ananya? Please don't say no. I want Sahil to move on, and only then will he forget about his past."

"Ok, sir, I will try my best."

"I know it's tough, but I have seen the way you deal with him," saying this he left me agog. A girl for Sahil—my Sahil.

Right then Zoya entered the room and saw me standing mortified. She was gaping at me when I turned to her and asked, "Zoya , can I borrow your clothes?" I knew how to bring Sahil to the party. "Yes why not? I will be more than happy if you wear any of my dresses and avoid your jeans to the party."

"Show me the sexiest dress you have." Zoya gave me a horrified look.

"Will you wear it?"

"I used to wear dresses like those very often before I joined the office."

She opened her cupboard and pulled out piles of short dresses.

I choose a peach coloured bodycon with thin straps that enhanced my every curve reaching half way to my thighs. I teamed it up with my nude high heels. I left my long traces flowing, which reached my waist and twisted the sides to pin them up. After a long time, I put some light make up on and here I was ready for the party. Zoya looked at me with her open mouth. "Ananya....you are looking so gorgeous and sexy. Natasha and Kavya are gonna die seeing you like this."

"You are also looking beautiful Zoya," I replied. She was wearing a light green off shoulder dress.

"Let's go now. Sahil sir will not be able to take his eyes off you," She played naughty and for the first time I blushed. I wanted to tell her it's for him I have dressed up, because seeing me like this he was bound to attend the party to look after me. I knew if he still cared, he will rage with anger seeing me dressed like this and not let me go on my own.

We reached the party mansion in a bus that Samar had booked. I saw Kavya and Natasha looking toward me, now believing what they saw. Manoj looked towards me and swallowed before he said, "Ananya you look...I mean you are so beautiful."

"Thanks Manoj. You can now stop staring."

"Sorry. I have sent your photo to Ritvik."

I didn't have time to give that much thought. I was waiting for Sahil. My plan won't work if he will not see me. I remembered I had his number so I quickly smsed him; 'Come down and see how old I look in my short dress' I knew the words 'short dress' would do the trick. Samar saw me and had a similar expression as everyone else, "Ananya, you look ravishing," He looked at his wife for approval. "Wow! Where were you hiding your beauty for so long?" asked Ridhima."

"Did you talk to Sahil?" asked Samar.

"Yeah, he will be here in a minute." And there was he standing on the top stair and looking around for me. He was looking so handsome in his dark blue shirt which was tight enough to show his worked out chest, the sleeves of the shirt were small and folded upside with a small black button and he had teamed it up with his black denims and blue shoes matching his shirt. I could see how girls were not able to take their eyes off my Sahil. Sahil finally spotted me and came down towards us, but was interrupted by Kavya and Natasha. They wanted to say something but he moved away from them, to us. His eyes were just on me, tracing me from top to bottom and burning with anger. He looked at me but asked Samar, "Bhai, can I come to the party too?

"Of course!" Samar stuttered with excitement.

"Sahil you are looking so handsome." "Thank you, Bhabhi," He said without a smile and then looked at me and said, "But some people have completely lost their dressing sense,"

Samar looked at me questioningly. Then he asked, "Sahil you want to go on the bus or you are coming in our car?"

"No bhai, I will be taking my car." Sahil came towards me and held my hand and said, "*Chalo*".

I freed my hand from him and said, "I'm going on the bus." Sahil kept both his hands on his hips and looked at me with anger. "I'm not letting you go on that bus, when you are wearing this awful dress. Either change your dress or come along with me; choice is yours."

Samar and Ridhima were looking at us in utter shock. Zoya was shell shocked as well. "Ananya, you go with Sahil," said Ridhima. I agreed reluctantly. One look at Samar's face and I knew he knew that Sahil feels something special for me. Sahil opened the door and I sat in front, the dress was really short as It trailed more up barring my thighs further and I was regretting wearing it. I kept pulling it down but to no avail. Sahil looked at me and then my exposed thighs and thundered, "Why did you wear such a dress?"

"You better look in front while driving and stop commenting on my dress. It was you who said I have poor dressing sense. Now look at the other women and tell me."

"I'm not concerned about any other women Ananya!" He screamed at the top of his voice. We reached the disc and before entering, Sahil took my hand in his and held it tightly. "Sahil leave my hand."

"No, I will not," and he tightened his grip. "I'm not letting you go anywhere without me." "Sahil, please stop this nonsense."

"I know you wore this dress just to irritate me."

"It's my wish. I can wear whatever I want," and I jerked away my hand from his hand and said, "You have no right to hold my hand as you have already left me long time back," And I dashed into the disc leaving him alone.

The place was quite noisy and dark. People were dancing on the dance floor like crazy.

I saw my colleagues sitting on the right, on the sofa. Manoj signalled me to join all of them. I made my way towards them and sat with Zoya and Manoj. Sahil sat with Samar on the other side, but his eyes were just on me. Kunal, one of the trainees, who was constantly staring at me came to me and asked, "Ananya ma'am, can I dance with you?" I was in no mood to dance, as it was Sahil who was going in my mind and the girl who was about to come to meet him. "Sorry Kunal, not today please." He went back disappointed. A beautiful tall girl in her early twenties walked towards Samar. She had long hair like me, but they were coloured golden yellow unlike mine and she had left them open. She was wearing a knee length long navy blue dress with high heels and light make up with dark red lipstick. Samar stood up greeting her and kissing her on her cheeks.

Oh shit! She is the girl whom Samar wanted to meet Sahil. Bad choice Samar bhaiya. Her dark lipstick will be the biggest turn off for my Sahil. He hated me when I used to put darker shades on my lips and he used to always wipe it with the tissue paper. Sahil stood up and shook hands with her but his eyes were just on me. Samar and Ridhima stood up and came towards me leaving Sahil and that girl alone. " Hey everyone! Ananya, I did not know Sahil was so possessive about his friends," Said Ridhima smiling.

I could only return a smile in answer. "That's my friend's sister. Her name is Jaanvi. She just came back from New York and has studied business," Explained Samar when he saw me looking at Sahil and that new girl. My face fell when I saw Sahil showcasing his cute dimples and making the girl blush scarlet. I knew he was doing this on purpose now to tease me.

I thought, Sahil stop playing with her feelings, but suddenly he stood up and took Jhanvi's hand and led her to the dance floor which was so unlike Sahil. I remember how he used to make excuses to not dance and it was I who used to force him to dance. My heart broke into several pieces, but why was I feeling bad for myself, did I still haves feeling for him? No, I hated him after what he did to me. But Samar was elated to see Sahil on the dance floor. Kavya came and spitted her venom, "Oh feeling bad? What were you thinking? You will wear a dress like that and attract him? How many boys do you want!? Is Ritvik not enough for you?"

"Kavya just get lost!" I screamed. I could see Sahil dancing with Jahnvi on a slow song twirling her around placing both his hands on her waist while she came forward to him ,but he quickly moved out of her grip and looked at me nervously and this time I faced the other side, wiping my tears.

"Why don't you go and tell Sahil sir that you still love him?"

"I don't love him Zoya. I just hate him; please leave me alone for some time." I was not able to hold back my tears. I don't know why I was feeling so bad, seeing Sahil dancing with that New York return. Kunal came to me with a glass of orange juice, "Ananya ma'am, everything all right?

"Yeah, I'm just not feeling my best."

"Don't worry ma'am, you can have this glass of juice and you will feel better."

"No, it's ok. I will take one myself."

"Please ma'am, don't say no, it's only a juice."

I took the glass to not offend him and drank it in one go. It left a bitter taste in my mouth afterward. "Why does it taste bad?" I asked Kunal.

After sometime I could feel my head spinning hard. I looked around but could not find Zoya. I could feel a weird sensation throughout my whole body.

I stood up and was about to fall that Kunal came and held me from behind. I could feel his hands on my stomach holding me tight. I quickly pushed him aside and said, "Don't you dare touch me." I walked and bumped into Manoj who gave me a shocked look.

"Oh, sorry Manoj," I sluttered and laughed and pulled his cheeks and said, "Are you ok?" Manoj pushed my hands away and said, "Ananya you are drunk! I did not know you were into drinking." I ignored him and asked, "Manoj, have you seen my Sahil?" He looked at me with his eyes wide. "Ananya, you are not in your senses. What are you talking and why are you calling him as your Sahil? What will Samar say when they hears you talk such nonsense?"

I ignored what he said and held his hand and said, "Please Manoj, don't be so mean. Can't you tell me where is he." Manoj jerked his hand away from mine and said, "Ananya don't ruin your career." Kavya took her chance and to instigate me pointed out to where Sahil was. I giggled like a teenager and made my way towards Sahil. I was tipsy but not tripping. "Ananya you are badly drunk! Careful there! You want me to take you home?' Asked Samar concerned. "Samar bhaiya," I screamed to get him to hear me above the loud music. "What the hell is your problem? He looked shocked. "Why do you always come between me and Sahil?"

"What do you mean?"

"Where is my Sahil?" I asked like an idiot.

Samar was angry now. "First of all he is not your Sahil and don't get so involved with him. He is with Jhanvi. If you helped out that does not mean you will cross your limit and talk to me like this. I asked you if are you serious about Sahil and you said that its nothing between the two of you. So I talked to Jhanvi and now everything is going fine. Sahil is mixing up with her and you want to ruin everything! Just stay away from Sahil."

"Wow Samar bhaiya! You are telling me to stay away from him again. No! I will not stay away from him this time. He is mine…only mine! Do you get that? And I'm not going to share him with any woman and Sahil does not evenlike that girl. I know him; he is just pretending and doing it deliberately to make me jealous."

"And how can you be so sure Ananya?" Asked Samar radiating with anger.

"Because Samar bhaiya, Sahil don't like women wearing dark lipsticks and having coloured hair," And I started giggling.

"Have you totally lost it!? What rubbish are you talking and when did I stopped you from talking to Sahil? I wanted you both to come together and you are saying that I asked you to stop talking to him?" He looked at me surprised. I was crying. "Are you happy now Samar bhaiya? See how you have damaged your brother's life. I wish you had fought for us, or supported Sahil and not let him break down. 'Anu just stay away from my brother. He is getting married tomorrow, so please just go away. I can't help you guys anymore, please you also move on.' That's what you said to me. Samar stood frozen. Ridhima held my hand and said, "Enough Ananya, I'm not letting you ruin Sahil's evening."

"Let her go Ridhima. Don't stop her today," Said a moist-eyed Samar. "She is right. I wish I had more courage for myself and my brother and could stand against my father. I was weak." "Samar what are you saying?" Asked Ridhima innocently. "I will tell you later, just let Ananya go to Sahil right now."

"But Samar, she will talk nonsense in front of Jhanvi."

"Jhanvi is not meant for Sahil. She is right, my brother is just intentionally doing it."

I moved quickly, leaving both of them and called Sahil. He just ignored me and kept on talking to Jhanvi. I just went ahead and pushed Jhanvi a little and clung tightly to Sahil like a baby, shocking them both. Sahil tried to push me a little, but I clasped him tighter and looked towards Jhanvi. "Who the hell is she?" Asked Jhanvi exasperated.

"Jhanvi, he is my boyfriend and so please keep your hands off him. And you, how dare you touch her when I'm there for you?" Sahil looked at me wide eyed. "What nonsense is this Sahil, did your brother call me here to insult me?"

"No Jhanvi, I'm sorry. She is drunk and doesn't even know what she is saying."

I faced Sahil, held his face in my hands and kissed him on his lips, leaving him out of breath and before he could say anything more. Jhanvi stormed out in anger, and once again I giggled like a baby before saying, "*Chalo*, dance with me," I ordered Sahil. "Anu", he called me by that name for the first time in a long time, "Who got you drunk?"

I giggled, "I'm a big girl. Come on now! Are you dancing with me or should I dance with that Kunal?"

"Who is Kunal?"

"He is my trainee and he is so sweet. He brought orange juice for me. Please dance with me." But Sahil was on the verge to burst with anger. He dragged me from the dance floor. We passed across Samar and he tried to stop Sahil but he just dragged me to the place where my colleagues were sitting.

"Zoya," he called. "Just take care of her for a minute." She came running towards me while I giggled like a baby. "Manoj," called Sahil, "Tell me who the hell is Kunal?"

"What happened, Sahil? He is our trainee."

"Just answer me Manoj. Where the hell is he?" Manoj was all shaken up. "I'm asking you something!" And then Kunal came out trembling from between the crowd. Seeing him Sahil laid a strong punch on his face. "Sahil!!" Shouted Samar. "Zoya gave me some water please. Oh gosh! Why is Sahil fighting?" I tried to stand up but Zoya stopped me, "Ananya please don't go there. You are drunk."

Meanwhile Sahil was grabbing Kunal's collar tightly, asking him, "What did you put in Ananya's drink? Tell me or else I will hand over you to the police." Kunal shivered and said, "I'm sorry sir. I mixed alcohol in her juice."

Sahil slapped him tight and said to Manoj, "Manoj, I want this boy out of the project. Little did he realise that he was screaming. "Control yourself Sahil," Said Samar grabbing his shoulder. "We can deal with this Kunal tomorrow in the office. Don't create a scene here. Go and take care of Ananya. She needs you right now."

"Yeah bhai, I'm taking her home." Sahil came towards me in anger, help me stood up, put his hands around my waist and dragged me out of that creepy place making everybody look in astonishment. "I told you to take care of yourself Ananya, and don't you dare wear clothes like this. Do you do these kinds of silly things in Delhi as well?"

I don't know what came over me or maybe it was the influence of the alcohol but I just went close to him and hugged him tight. He was taken aback by my gesture, but he did not push me away this time rather slowly placed his one hand on my lower back and the other on my upper back and hugged me tightly gripping me in his tight embrace and we were standing hugging each other, when Samar made a throaty sound to make us aware of his presence. Sahil left me and moved away slightly. "Sahil you forgot your keys with me."

"Thanks bhai," He held my hand again and made me sit in the car. My body was burning with the liquor and my head was as heavy as if I was carrying a mountain on it. "Are you okay?" Asked Sahil while driving?

"My head hurts."

"Did you not realize there was something in your drink."

"No," I said, holding my head. "You know very well I don't drink."

"Precisely why I call you a baby. You are never careful; anybody can take advantage of you."

"Like you did," I retaliated and giggled like a baby.

"I have never ever taken advantage of you Ananya and you also know this."

He stopped the car in front of my pad. I tried to step out of the car, but was not able to hold myself as my head was spinning hard. Sahil came around and held me tightly.

"Leave me." I commanded pushing him away.

"Ananya you can't even stand on your own," And he pulled me close to him in his arms and led me to my room. I used to love this; being in his strong arms, caressing my back softly. I really missed him and at that moment of time I was really liking to be in his arms. I felt like hugging him tightly and kissing him to infinity—my Sahil.

"Give me the keys," He ordered and I started giggling again, "Keys are with Zoya."

"What!? Said an exasperated Sahil, still holding me. "What the hell Ananya? Why you did not tell me before?"

"You did not ask me before," And I giggled again. "No problem, we can sit here, under the sky full of stars and the cool breeze," And then I kissed him on his cheeks. "Ananya stop it." He retreated backwards.

"Why? Don't you like it anymore?"

"Miss Ananya, you are drunk right now and when you will come in your senses you are gonna regret it." And he dragged me to the big house

"No way am I going to your room."

"Ananya please come. You need rest," He tried to pull me but I resisted, so he picked me up in his arms. Wow! He pushed open the door of his room and made me stand while he switched on the light. His room was painted off white in colour the same colour of the room down stairs. There was a big mahagony bed in the middle of the room with light blue printed bedsheet. In front of the bed there was a big TV hanging on the wall and on the right side there was a big wooden shelf which was full of books. My bookholic Sahil, I smirked. "Come here," He pulled me towards the bed. "Why do you need such a big bed, Sahil? And I pulled his cheeks. He gave me his not so funny expression.

"Ananya, I knew some day you will be coming here drunk and would need to sleep. That's why I bought a big bed."

"Hmmm, nice choice," And I started unzipping my dress.

"What are you doing?" Sahil shouted like a manic.

"Just changing my dress Sahil. I'm feeling uncomfortable," And turning towards him I went close to him and started unbuttoning his dark blue shirt. He held my hand and shook me saying, "Come to your senses, Ananya."

"I want to wear your shirt, as every drunk girl wears it in the movies," I said innocently.

"No," he commanded. You are not doing any such stupidity. This is not a movie and you can sit in this dress for a while."

"Are you afraid of me?" I laughed.

"Yes, I'm," He said. You are out of control."

"I have lost all my senses after meeting you again," I said and walked towards him again, making him sense that he cannot stop me. "Anu..." He said, but I placed my finger on his lips and said, "Shhhh Sahil...You know na I hate you so much."

"Yeah, I know," He said looking into my eyes with a guilty expression. I held his neck gently with both my hands and pulled his face down and looking into his eyes said, "Hold me, Sahil."

He stood frozen. I moved my one hand from his neck and held his hands, one by one and place them on my lower back. He was staring me into my eyes now. I scrunched my feet up and Sahil's grip became tighter around my waist. I ran my finger across his chin, dimples and then his lips kissing him on his forehead like the way he used to kiss me always, and then I kissed my favourite place, his cute dimples and made him look at me with tears in his eyes. It was difficult for me to control myself any further and so, I kissed him on his lips, brushing my soft lips against his, just remembering my love for him. I kissed him like never before. He resisted the torture, not responding and making me feel rejected again. I was not looking into his eyes now, but I was holding him from his biceps.

He kept his hand on my face and held it and kissed me on my forehead and pained, he said, "Ananya, you are drunk. You don't know what you are doing."

"I know what I want right now, Sahil." I said looking into his eyes. He looked at me for a second thinking something and then he kissed me slowly and softly making every nerve of my body crave for more and more. We kissed each other for a long time as none of us wanted to stop. But finally when we did stop, finding each other out of breath, Sahil embraced me again in his tight hug, and then picked me up in his arms and made me lay down on his bed and covered my bare legs with a soft blanket but I held his hands tighter. I didn't want him to leave me. "You also sleep with me please, don't go."

"Anu ..Please don't make things difficult for us," But without answering him I pulled him and forced him to lay on the bed with me. "Anu when you will wake up, you will break my head," I smiled and rested my head over his chest, my arm on his arms while his arm came around mine and he started stroking my hair softly. I don't know when I slept.

Chapter 20

I woke up with a severe headache. Sahil's hand was on my stomach and his lips were resting close to my ears. I was still in his room. "Oh God Sahil!" I shouted, making him sit up with a jolt. "Why am I sleeping here with you?" I remembered only a few things. I had got drunk. The fight. Sahil holding my hand. But that was all. "What did we do last night!?" I asked. There was panic written all over my face.

"We did nothing Ananya. You were drunk. You were not letting me go anywhere and you asked me to sleep here with you. Nothing happened. I did not do anything. We just slept together."

"No! I don't trust you anymore!" I screamed and tears came rolling down my cheeks.

"I knew this is what was going to happen in the morning!" Said Sahil slapping his forehead.

"Anu…" He tried to cajole. "We did nothing last night for which you should be ashamed of except…."

"Except?" I looked in his eyes terrified. "Except what?"

"We kissed each other."

"What! No! You are lying," I said placing my hands on my lips. "Sahil I was drunk, but you were okay. How did you let it happen?"

"Anu, you kissed me first and you were so upset because I did not reciprocate and you were adament, so I kissed you. I'm sorry."

"Sorry!? What are you asking sorry for Sahil? I know how long your single kiss lasts," He blushed showing me his cute dimples.

"Why can't I remember anything?"

"You want me to remind you?" He teased.

"Just don't act smart. I was drunk. It won't happen again," I retorted.

He smirked and walked past me closing the washroom door.

A while later he came out wiping his face with a towel, "You want to use the washroom?"

He got alarmed seeing me with my hand on my head. "What happened? Headache?" He asked.

"No, I am thinking how will I go down now? It's so embarrassing."

"Don't worry nobody is downstairs. They all came around 1 at night and today is Saturday, everybody must be sleeping."

"I'm going down before anybody gets to know I spent the whole night with you and that too without doing anything."

"Oh, so you regret not doing anything with me?" He was smiling.

I gave him a cold stare and started to walk out. "Wait I'm also coming," And we walked together out of the room.

Sahil was right nobody was there on the breakfast table, except Samar who was sitting and reading the newspaper. Shit! before I could hide behind Sahil, he saw me. Without looking at Samar I was about to leave but he stopped me. "How are you feeling today?"

"I'm better," I said, without looking at him. I remembered I had told him that I was Anu. "We will take strict action against Kunal. Don't worry." He commented.

"He needs to be thrown out of the company," Said Sahil.

"No, please don't do that. It will ruin his life," I said worried.

"No need to be so empathetic, Ananya. You don't even know what *tamasha* you created there."

"Oh no!", I said seeing Natasha and tried to leave but Sahil held my hand and pulled me back. "Why do you bother so much about them?"

"Because they are crazy for you and they have given me warning to stay away from you."

"It seems my brother is in high demand," Joked Samar. "Don't worry now, Ananya. Everybody saw you announcing on the floor last night that Sahil is your's." My mouth half opened drowning me in the ocean of embarrassment.

Sahil gave Samar a cold stare but did not said anything. "I'm so sorry Samar sir. I don't remember what all did I say, but whatever I said it was under the influence of alcohol and if I have hurt you, please forgive me. It was not intentional."

"Hey, don't worry Ananya, you said nothing that you should be so ashamed of. It's ok; not your fault. The culprit needs to be punished."

I bowed my head and made a move. Sahil decided to walk along with me. We walked passed Kavya and Natasha who were staring at us. "I'm sorry," I said to Sahil, "for all that happened yesterday."

"Which part? I know it was a bit embarrassing there on the disc, but I liked the way you declared that I'm yours and no other women will touch me and I liked when we both were…" "Sahil please," I cut him short, "All that happened under the influence of alcohol. I still remember how you left me. I just hate you. Please don't give yourself any false hope."

"Ok," he said, "I know, go and take some rest now."

I was having a severe headache and was relieved to see Zoya sleeping. She looked up when I entered and asked, "Hey Ananya, how are you feeling and where were you?

"You had the keys so Sahil made me sleep in the guest room." I lied as I did not want her to think too much.

Day passed in a daze and around night there was a knock at my door. I opened it to see Sahil standing there. He pushed the door wide open and came inside all serious and latched the door.

"Why are you latching the door?" I panicked.

"Because I want to kiss you again,"

"What!? Have you gone mad?"

"Silly girl. Come on, get ready. I'm hungry."

"I am not! Please don't create a scene in front of my colleagues."

"I don't care about them."

"But I do."

He gave me a look and I knew he was not going to budge so I quickly changed and announced, "Let's go." He looked at me from top to toe and remarked, "You can't live without your jeans."

"Stop commenting on my clothes," and I switched off the lights.

We entered the room together and thankfully there were only a few people left.

Zoya gave me a quizzical smile and I was about to go there to sit with her, but Sahil held my hand and said, "Not there, we will sit here."

"Oh no Ananya, who brought you here? Me. So you will sit with me."

"Sahil grow up. Stop being a baby."

"That is your job being a baby, but someday I would love to baby sit you." He said smiling.

"Hey Ananya!" Called Ridhima when we sat on the chair. "What was the joke? Share with us."

I was so embarrassed, so I said, "Sahil will tell you ma'am." Sahil choked on the glass of water which he was drinking…spitting a little on the table a little. "Sahil its okay. I will not ask you about the joke, I know it was meant only for you both." And Samar and Ridhima started laughing making us go pale.

"Anyway, Sahil what's your plan this weekend? Monday is also a holiday. Let's go out for two days somewhere," Said Ridhima excited.

"I don't want to go."

"Sahil you had not taken any break since a long time. What will you do here? We are going to our farm house. Ananya please ask him to come along with us."

"Yes Sahil, you should go and I will also be at peace for two days."

Samar heard me and stifled a laugh. "Of course, you will ask me and I will go. Right Ananya?" Asked Sahil.

"Ananya can also join us!" Said Ridhima smiling purposefully. Now we looked at each other shocked. Me going to their farm house! "No, I can't go," I said. "Oh Ananya, please don't say no. It will be fun and don't worry Sahil will not bother you."

"Ananya I don't want to listen to anything," Samar also added. "You both are coming with us. We will be leaving in the morning at 5, so be ready in time." "What!? 5 in the morning!" I asked again to confirm. Sahil laughed and said, "Bhai, you can't wake her up at 5 unless you are screaming in her ears." I accepted the challenge.

I woke up at 4.30 as I knew he will tease me later if I got late and I quickly dressed up in a one piece, pink, sleeveless, knee length dress with a high neck collar and two strings to tie at the back. I was still undecisive to go. I was about to call Samar to say I can't go, but Zoya stopped me and said, I think you should go and spend some time with Sahil to know what exactly is going on in his mind."

I stepped out and saw Sahil coming out alone from the big house. He was looking handsome in his black tee and khakhi pants and his beautiful smile. For a moment I thought of our kiss.

He came towards me and blurted, "Wanted to kiss me again, Anu?" I gasped, how did he make out? I raised my eyebrow and said, "In your dreams." He laughed and said, "There, I do every night."

"Just shut up and look, I'm ready before time. Where are Samar and Ridhima?"

"They will come a little late. You are coming with me."

"What? I don't want to get bored with you."

"Oh come on, Anu. I know you were dying to spend time with me."

"Start your car now before I change my mind."

"I won't let you change your mind," He said grinning. We did not talk much in the car. He stopped his car in front of a big gate which was carved with golden leaves and painted black from beneath. Parking the car in front of the gate we got off. He pressed the bell and a guard came out and said, "Hello Sahil sir." For some reason he was horrified to see me with him. Sahil took the keys from him and said, "Samar is on his way." The guard relaxed to know that we were not alone. We walked across a stony path which had big trees and beautiful potted flowers. "Wow, this is exquisite," I said. "I did not know you are so rich," I teased him. "This belongs to my dad," He said seriously. "Oh, and how is he?"

"He died last year due to his increased drinking problem."

"I'm so sorry Sahil."

"No it's ok we both did not share a good relation because of his interfering nature, but still he was my dad and I miss him. Anyways, here we are..." And he opened the lock of the door. It had a big drawing room with flower pots kept in every corner and a centre table kept in the middle, which was black in colour, and I could see there were four doors on each side, they must be the rooms as there was no staircase. "It is not as big from inside as nobody lives here, but we come here often. My father was very fond of this place. He bought it for my mother. Lot of emotions are involved in this and that's why we don't sell it. You want something to drink?" Asked Sahil, changing the topic.

"Yes," I said, "Maybe water."

"Oh, I thought you will say you want a drink," He raised his eyebrows teasing me.

"Just shut up Sahil and give me some water."

"Ordering the boss?" He raised an eyebrow in mock disapproval.

"You are not my boss. I'm working in a team with you and I will go back soon." His expression changed from happy to sad. "Ok, sit please," He said and went inside the kitchen with a straight face. Even I was feeling bad I don't know why. No, I need to be brave and not let those emotions come back which had hurt me so much but I really felt bad for his dad. He had ruined his and his children's life, just because he was not lucky in love. Placing the glass of water in front of me, Sahil sat down on the chair facing me. "Stop staring, Sahil."

"I'm not staring. I was just looking at how much you have changed."

"What do you mean by changed?"

"You look more mature now."

"Are you trying to say I am old now?"

His lips curled into a smile. "Why didn't you marry?"

"It's none of your business, Sahil. Did I asked you why your ex-wife is so mad at you? His smile vanished and he said, "You can ask me and I will tell you."

"No. I'm least interested and don't annoy me with your boring talks. But I really wanted to know about Reem; where is she?" Smile came to his face, but did not reach his eyes.

"She stays in a hostel as she does not want to stay with Ridhima as she is Samar's second wife."

"So Samar bhaiya divorced Reem's mother."

"No, they patched up for Reem and they were even happy with each other, but Reem's mother was diagnosed with cancer 3 years back and we lost her."

"Reem was so shaken up by the incident that she had to take treatment for depression, and she is not very comfortable with Ridhima bhabhi, though she is very nice and caring, but she is not able to bond with her."

"But she was close to you. Why did you let her go to the hostel?"

"She still is close to me but I was staying at Hyderabad because of my ex-wife and she used to create a chaos if Reem was around."

I was crest fallen hearing this about Reem. Our talk was interrupted by a door bell.

It must be Samar. We both rose from our seats.

"Hey!" Said Ridhima, "I hope Sahil did not scare you."

"Not at all. I scare him."

Samar laughed a hearty laugh and said, "Ananya only you can control him." Sahil wasn't pleased and retorted, "Bhai please, I'm not a baby to be controlled, rather she is. Anyway you both can freshen up, then we can have breakfast together."

When they left, Sahil got me back and asked, "Okay. So, why didn't you marry?"

I was quite for a moment. "Why do you want to know?"

"I just want to know," said my annoying Sahil.

"You are asking me this Sahil? You left me without even meeting me one last time and talking to me, and then I got the news that you are getting married.

I was devastated, my parents took me back when they came to know about all this.

Seeing me broken they were also broken. It took me a long time to come out of all this, and you are asking me why I did not get married?"

Sahil was quite not looking in my eyes.

"I'm sorry Ananya I know I had punished you really hard but circumstances were such that I had to marry her."

"Sahil you could have told me once. I would have done something."

"It was of no use Ananya. My father was adamant and I did not have enough courage to bid you goodbye; I would have broken in front of you."

"Sahil just tell me one thing; I have been thinking of this for the past five years—Did you ever love me?" Now he looked me in my eyes and I could see the guilt and pain in his. "I have always loved you Anu. My love was not fake. I loved you so much that I was never able to love Manyata. I tried to, but it was you who was always in my heart. I was not able to forget you and this is the main reason Manyata left me. I left no choice for her." I knew he was not lying. I could see pain in his eyes, but still it was not so easy for me to forget all the pain which I had gone through in these five years.

"Guys, breakfast is ready," said Ridhima.

"We need to go back tomorrow," Said Samar finishing his breakfast.

"But you said we are gonna stay for two days."

"Actually, I got a call from the office, I need to be there tomorrow."

"All well bhai?"

"Yeah, don't worry. Let's enjoy our today."

I rose up and asked Sahil where my room was. He gave me a quizzical look and said, "You mean our room?" "Excuse me Sahil, I meant my room. Who said I'm sharing the room with you?" "Anu you already have shared room with me and remember you were the one eager to sleep resting on my chest." "Oh yes, and when I woke up, your hand was on my stomach, that showed your eagerness." He grinned, showing all his teeth, "Come, I'll show you your room." He took me to one.

"This is your room and the next one is mine. So if you are afraid sleeping alone, my door will be open. You can come in anytime."

"Get lost!" He still loved teasing me.

I layed down and pondered over the conversation between me and Sahil.

He had said he had always loved me and he was not able to love Manyata, but what about their daughter? I woke up with a knock on my room. I went and opened the door rubbing my eyes. "You were sleeping. It's 1 in the afternoon. I was joking and you took it seriously."

"So what? I woke up at 4.30 in the morning." Sahil pushed me aside and entered my room.

"Who gave you the permission to come inside?"

"It's my house sweety. I don't need your permission."

"Irritating monster!" I buzzed.

"I heard it. Get ready soon, we are going out. Bhai is waiting for us. We have not come here to sleep."

"Ok so get out and let me get ready."

"I'm not going out. I know you will sleep again. There is a washroom. You can change there."

"Why do you have to be so irritating all the time?"

After taking our lunch we roamed around and shopped a little. By the end we were tired and so went to a nearby restaurant to pack ourselves with some energy. It was a beautiful place. with light music and beautiful ambience. Every table was separated with a brown shield to provide privacy to the guest.

We sat at a corner table. Samar and I on one side and Ridhima and Samar in front of us. "If you want to have dinner separately, you guys can carry on, we won't mind." Said Ridhima smiling.

We looked at each other and Sahil said, "Bhabhi I want to enjoy my dinner, she just knows how to fight, while at the same time I said, "Everybody here knows Sahil, who is a fighter."

Samar smiled and said, "You both are fighting like a married couple."

Embarrassed, we looked down. "So, what shall we order?" Asked Samar looking towards us. "Hey, let's play a game and make our day memorable. I will order Samar's favourite food and Ananya will order Sahil's favourite food and then let us see if we were right or wrong," Quipped Ridhimaa

Sahil gave me an uncomfortable look, "But bhabhi she doesn't know of my choices."

"Oh, come on Sahil, you said you both were friends for some time, so this much Ananya must be knowing about you. She won't be punished of she doesn't get it right."

"But even if I guess it right, Sahil will say it's not."

"Don't worry Ananya. We both know his favourite is—it's the one dish every time."

"Oh, come on!" Said an exasperated Sahil. Everyone started laughing.

"Sahil, you should enjoy these little things," Said Ridhima.

"Yeah, she is right," I smiled and looked at Sahil. I knew I was going to win because I knew what he liked to eat. "What if I win,?" I asked Samar and Ridhima.

Ridhima thought for a while and said, "A gift from the other party."

"I will give you a night suit," Commented Sahil slowly. I looked at him squinting my eyes, and I could see Ridhima and Samar trying to stifle their laughs. "Okay guys, let's start. Ridhima it's your turn first."

"Rajma rice and shahi paneer," Said Ridhima, smiling. Samar grinned and kissed her on her forehead. Sahil looked at me and mouthed, "Don't even think."

"Hah!" I mouthed back. "You guys talk in code words," Said Ridhima, "Anyway you both can carry on later. Ananya it's your turn." Without picking up the menu card, I said, "He will have Manchurian fried rice with extra ginger and red chilli, served with a bowl of curd. Samar and Ridhima were shocked to hear me. Sahil put his hand on his neck and faced the other side smiling. "Wow Ananya! You really know him well," Said Ridhima. To Sahil she cooed, "Awww Sahil, you lost. Now you have to give a beautiful gift to Ananya."

"I will," Said Sahil, looking at me. Then he intentionally placed his hand on my back and kissed me on my forehead just the way Samar had kissed Ridhima, snatching words away from my mouth.

"Awww... you guys are so cute together," Said Ridhima and I could see the happiness on Samar's face. I knew Sahil did it on purpose and I felt like breaking his head.

After our dinner was finished and we were having some ice cream, Samar looked up and asked me, "So what is your future plan?"

"Nothing in particular. Just work on interesting projects."

"So where do your parents live?" Asked Ridhima.

"They live in Jaipur."

"It must be difficult to stay far from your parents."

"Yeah, it is, but you need to sacrifice something to be something in life."

"So, any plans for marriage?" Asked Samar eyeing me and Sahil.

My spoon was left hanging midway and Sahil's just fell on the ground. "Sorry," He said.

"I will be married off by the end of this year; my mother has searched somebody for me."

There was silence for a second as if they heard the news of somebody's death.

I could see Samar's face all pale, devoid of any emotion. "So, you are happy to spend your life with a person whom you don't know?" Asked Ridhima.

"We can know each other later on. Actually my mom doesn't trust my choice anymore after the person who

I was in love with left me for another woman without even telling me. So now I have decided to marry the boy of my mother's choice as I know he will not leave me." Sahil pushed his ice cream cup on the table and rose up and said, "I'm leaving now; you guys carry on with your stupid talks."

"Sahil, where are you going?" Called Samar but he did not reply.

I immediately regretted for what I had said.

We came back to the farm house, but Sahil had not reached yet. Samar tried to call him but his phone was switched off. "Where has this boy gone?" Said Samar, infuriated?

I know Samar was angry with me. He came to the couch where I was sitting and said, "I know you are upset with Sahil and me but Sahil has just loved you all his life. He was forced to marry that girl because of my father. You don't even know what all he has gone through in these 5 years."

Chapter 21

It was 12 in the night and Sahil had not returned, even I began to panic now. Where could he be? He was so happy in the morning and now he was again sad, just because of me. I could not stop the tears flowing from my eyes.

Ridhima saw me crying. She came immediately and hugged me and said, "Hey it's ok. Don't worry. We are used to this kind of behaviour. He often comes late when he is upset about something."

"I'm sorry ma'am. It's because of me that he is upset."

"Ananya, don't blame yourself," Said Samar coming towards me; just because of you we were able to see our old carefree Sahil. I don't understand, when you guys still care so much for each other, why are you both not able to put your past behind.?

"I know you both had gone through a lot and I cannot feel that pain of yours but I can relate to it. Sahil tried his level best to convince papa to marry you, he even stopped eating and was hospitalised, but our father, he was not at all affected rather he tried to kill himself and blackmailed

Sahil to marry his friend's daughter Manyata who was already two months pregnant with her lover's child who had betrayed her so to save the grace of our father's friend Sahil married Manyata, but was never able to love her. Manyata gave birth to a girl Kiaara and that changed Sahil's life. There was happiness on his face again and he was busy with Kiaara the whole day while Manyata used to be out enjoying all the time. One day Manyata told that Kiaara's biological father wants to be back with them as he is sorry for whatever happened. We tried a lot to stop her, but instead of being grateful she blamed Sahil for not being a good husband. Seeing all this Sahil broke down completely and seeing this our father realised his mistake, but it was too late. Now Kiaara's case is going on as Sahil is not allowed to meet Kiaara. Anu, when you came back Sahil started changing; what we were not able to do, you did it. It's only you who can bring back his smile. I know it is not easy for you, but try to forget the past. He can only be happy with you." I could not say anything. Only tears rolled down my eyes. 'My Sahil he had gone through so much pain, but how do I let go my pain? What will I tell my parents? They will not agree to it now as they had seen my anguish for him.'

Five minutes later we heard a thud at the door, and Sahil came in drunk, pushing the door. Samar ran towards him and held him in his arms.

"Sahil, what is wrong with you? When will you learn to handle your rejections peacefully?" "Bhai just leave me," And he strode towards me. "Ananya ma'am, were you crying?" He laughed, "For whom? Not for me I guess. How can you cry for me, you don't care for me anymore. You are right, I'm a looser and the worst person on Earth. My fault is just whoever I love, never gets to be a part of my life. God takes away that person from me and makes me all alone."

I felt pity for my Sahil but I didn't know what to do. "Come," He held my hand and dragged me to his room, "I'll tell you today, why I left you." I looked at Samar and he came to my rescue, "Sahil, it's too late now and you are not in a position to talk right now. You can talk in the morning."

"No bhai I want to talk to her right now," And he was successful in dragging me to his room. But he was so drunk that he passed out as soon as he sat on his bed, holding my hand. I tried to pull my hand away from his grip, but it was tightly clasped in his hands

Samar came and made him lay on the bed properly and tried to unclasp my hand, but I didn't want to leave my Sahil alone in this condition.

"It's okay Samar bhaiya. Let it be. If you don't mind, can I spend some time with him?"

"Sure, you don't have to take my permission. Just take care of him. He is too broken."

I nodded and he left, leaving me and my Sahil alone. I kissed him on his forehead and placed my head over his chest and went off to sleep.

I heard a small voice in my sleep, "Anu, wake up, we need to go."

My Sahil was back in his senses waking me up. I was sleeping in his arms and didn't want to move out from it. I came closer to him, placed my head higher on his chest and kissed him on his cheeks. He enveloped me tightly and kissed me on my forehead stroking my back.

"Anu, what are you doing in my bed?" I looked at him and said "What to do? You were drunk and not letting me go." "I'm so sorry Ananya I should not have gotten drunk.

I sat up moving out of his grip and coming back to reality. "Yes, you should learn to control your anger, Sahil." We heard a knock on the door. "Sahil, we are leaving in 10 minutes. Are you guys coming with us or staying back?" Sahil looked at me and asked, "You want to stay back with me?" I longed to stay back in his arms for as long as he wanted, but didn't want to complicate the situation and hurt each other more.

I just shook my head and he sighed, "It's okay. I can understand."

"No bhai," He shouted, "We are coming with you." We both came out in 10 minutes.

"How are you feeling today, Sahil?" Asked Ridhima worried, "I'm fine now, bhabhi and sorry for yesterday." "Sahil you should say sorry to Ananya not me, she cried so much yesterday."

Sahil looked at me and asked, "Why do you hurt yourself because of me?"

"Sahil, I'm hungry. I don't want to talk about it."

We reached back around 2. Sahil parked the car outside my pad. "Sahil please don't drink," I said when he was about to go and he just nodded.

Next day when I reached office to see Sahil working on the final presentation which we were supposed to present today. He signalled me to sit down and we worked on our reports for three hours, without talking to each other. "Let's go," He said and moved out.

Sahil was to the point during his conversation and explained everything with aplomb. Our CEO was very pleased with the presentation. "Good job, Mr Sahil." "Thank you, sir, but it is a team effort. Miss Ananya helped me out a lot in this." "Hmm," he said looking towards me, "Well done, Miss Ananya. Keep up the good work."

Everybody moved out of the conference room, leaving me and Sahil alone. "Thank you for giving me half the credit," I said.

He gave me his notorious smile and said, "I would have done the same even if Natasha was there in your place." This was enough to make me go mad and I came out of the conference room staring at him which made him giggle some more.

After finishing my dinner, I went outside in the garden to get some fresh air. My life seemed like an unsolved puzzle to me. Why was I so affected with Sahil again, or was I still in love with him and can't see him go away from me? I was cursing myself for coming to Bangalore; it had taken me so long to forget Sahil and now my past was standing again in front of me.

When I got inside, Zoya was busy talking on the phone. I layed down on the bed, thinking about him; how Sahil used to curse me when I used to call him late at night, especially on his birthday. Oh God! it was 10 October tomorrow, how could I forget it was my Sahil's birthday? Then I realized not my Sahil anymore; when would I come in terms with that?

I know he will not celebrate his birthday and would shout at me if I wished him, but I really wanted to wish him on his birthday, when he was in front of me.

It was around 12 in the night and I was not able to sleep. Then I checked the date on my phone and it was 10 of October, Sahil's birthday. Zoya was talking on the phone with Vikram. Seeing me siting she at once disconnected the phone and asked me if all was well.

"Yeah, it's Sahil's birthday today."

"Oh, wow! So you should wish him Ananya. What are you waiting for?"

"No Zoya, he hates it when somebody calls him at midnight," And I told her about the incident when I wished him for the first time, making Zoya laugh, holding her stomach.

"Aww...really Sahil sir is so cute." I laughed. "Okay, not in that way. But I know many women are crazy just to get one look of him. But Ananya his eyes are always on you. I can see immense love and care for you. Then suddenly a wicked thought came into my mind, "But Zoya I would love to irritate him." "What do you mean?" "Yesterday he was not talking to me properly, now I will irritate him to insanity. Let's go to his room." "What!?" Shouted Zoya now. "No Ananya, don't be stupid. You can call him." "No, he will not pick up my phone I know him. He will not say anything to you and secondly, he looks damn cute with his ruffled hair when he is half asleep rubbing his eyes like a cute puppy." I could see the horror on Zoya's face, "Ananya, you are so mean and when did you see him like that?" She winked.

I dragged her out. "Ananya, you are turning wicked in love."

"Everything is fair in love and war." "Ananya are you going out in your night suit for the first time." I looked towards my bare legs as my night dress was above my knees and a big Mickey mouse was printed on it with a caption, I love to be a baby again.

"Oh shit! I need to change it." "It's ok Ananya, see I'm also wearing the same one like you but there is no Mickey mouse." "Oh, shut up Zoya." I didn't care about my night suit anymore.

We slowly went to the main hall and opened the door; thank God it was not locked.

"Ananya if somebody else saw us..." Even I was scared now, and don't know how would my angry man would behave seeing me in a funny piece. After entering the dining room Zoya asked me if I knew his room. "Second one from right," I told her

I knocked on the door and we both hid in the corner of the door. Sahil came out rubbing his eyes. I quickly held Zoya's hand pushed him aside and ran inside, making Sahil freeze for a moment. He was not wearing his shirt and Zoya was here in his room! I should have come alone. Sahil was still in a dilemma, so I whispered, "You can come in. It's your room."

Zoya closed her eyes and Sahil came inside closing the door with a bang. Thank god he did not switch on the light and only a dim yellow light was on, but how could I ignore his strong build body. I was staring while he was wearing his shirt. "Ananya, stop staring and say something," Said Zoya pushing me. "Zoya let's go back." I knew that my lion was super angry now and finally, he switched on the lights and sat on the edge of the bed looking at us. He stared at me from head to toe. After waiting for a while he narrowed his eyes and said, "You both dropped like a bomb in my room!"

He was right, so I stammered, "Zoya came to wish you happy birthday."

"What!?" Zoya paled and so I clutched her hand tightly. "Yaa right, I came to wish you, sir. Happy birthday sir." "Ananya doesn't think twice before doing stupid things, but you could have stopped her." It was enough for me now. "Excuse me," I shouted, "Sahil how dare you talk about me like this. I'm not a baby and see Zoya he is so mean, not even saying thank you to you."

"Ok fine," said Sahil, "Thanks Zoya and Ananya, you both have come here to wish me after taking so much risk. Now you both can leave." I wanted to irritate Sahil, so I made my way to his bed and sat in the centre taking a pillow on my lap, "I'm not going like this." He turned towards me and said, "You look quite tempting sitting on my bed and wearing that Mickey mouse dress," And then I could see his smile, "Ananya when will you grow up? You are still a baby." And both Sahil and Zoya started laughing.

My plan was not going on the right track. I came here to irritate him and he was not retaliating. "Sahil I want to watch tv as my return gift as there is no tv in our rooms." Now I was close to his annoyance. "Ananya enough is enough; please go out of my room right now." "Ananya lets go," Said Zoya getting scared.

"No, I said I'm not going anywhere is this the way to behave with the people who came to wish you on your birthday." "Ananya don't push me more." "No," I shouted "I want to watch tv right now." I demanded like a baby. "You call me baby na, now I will behave like a baby."

"Ok fine," Said Sahil and he looked towards Zoya and said, "Come, you should not ruin your night for her." "Zoya is not going anywhere without me." "No Ananya, I need to give you your return gift and I have a special one for you." He grinned. "Ohh shit!" I murmured. He had changed track. "You can give me in front of Zoya." "No Anu," He smiled again, "I don't want to embarrass Zoya," and he held her hand and took her out, locking me inside. I kept my hands on my head thinking, Oh gosh! What do I do now? I knew he was not gonna leave me now, I'm finished. By the time he came I was standing near his bed thinking of how to rescue myself. He locked the door from inside and started unbuttoning his shirt. "Hey, what are you doing?" I panicked. Leaving his shirt open and showing his sculpted body, he came towards me making me sweat. "Playing games with me, Miss Ananya?"

"Listen Sahil, I just came to wish you." He stood half an inch away from me making my heart beat trillions of time in a second.

He grabbed me from my waist and pulled me close to him. I could feel his breath now.

"Sahil please, leave me. Don't cross your limit. I just came to wish you, that's it."

"I know and that's why I'm giving you your return gift, which you asked from me."

"I did not ask for a kiss. I just asked to watch TV."

"Yeah, right Anu, we will watch TV, as you have ruined my sleep and now I will not let you sleep and you will go out from here in the morning."

"Oh please Sahil, you can't stop me. I'll complain to Samar." He scoffed and said, "You can do it Anu but remember he is my brother. Stop talking and kiss me now," He ordered. He was looking into my eyes now. "Anu it's my birthday gift please," he pleaded now.

"Sahil I will give you a present tomorrow." "No," he said in a firm voice, "I need it right now."

"Sahil stop being childish."

"Really, Ananya," and before I could push him any further, his lips were on mine, kissing me softly with much love and warmth. His grip was quite tight for me to move as he was holding me tightly against him, my hands were on his bare chest, stopping him from coming close but soon I lost the battle. I was blindfolded once again by my Sahil's love and charm, and to be honest, I was loving the way he was kissing me with so much love, so I finally gave in, moving my hands slowly from his chest and taking them upwards encircling his neck to pull him close to me, removing all the distance between both of us. He took a deep breath and made our kiss more passionate involving me into it completely to be the partner in crime, it was difficult for both of us to resist each other now. I could feel Sahil's hand on my leg, creeping up slowly. He had never touched me like this before but I didn't want him to stop, but I was not ready for such a big step and so I brought my hands back from his neck and placed on his bare chest once again indicating him to stop but he did not this time. My gentlemen Sahil vanished in front of this wicked Sahil. He held my hands and once again placed them on his neck without breaking the kiss and placed both his hands on my waist and then slowly finished the kiss and looked into my eyes .

Before I could say anything, he started kissing me on my neck slowly, lowering down on the strap on my shoulder and making his way downward. The feeling was enchanting but this torture was enough for me and finally I surrendered myself completely to my Sahil hugging him tightly and kissing him on his ear. His grip became tighter kissing me on my lips again and slowly deepening his kiss. I knew we had a long way to go as he picked me up in his arms and made me lie on his bed. I was not thinking of anything else except that I love this man so much that I was ready to give my everything to him. He took off his shirt and came over me resting his body on his elbows and kissed me on my forehead. We both looked into each other's eyes as to take permission from each other. I held his face bringing it closer and kissed him on his lips. He reciprocated with even more love and warmth. I could feel his weight on me now. He was mine, all mine, forever my Sahil. He kissed me all over my neck and collar bone lowering the strap again as he did a few minutes ago. I could feel immense love in his every single kiss, taking me to a different world, where nothing mattered, just our love for each other.

We both came to a halt when we heard a knock on the door and we pushed each other away.

There was panic in our eyes. He quickly picked up his shirt, buttoned it quickly and looked t me and said, "Anu you could have worn something decent." He quickly went to his cupboard, and threw one of his jackets from the cupboard and I wore it quickly. Sahil calmed himself down as he was out of breath now and opened the door.

"Surprise!" I could hear Ridhima and Samar's voice. "Happy birthday bhai!" Said Samar.

"Will you keep us standing here like this? Ridhima said and came inside the room. She saw me there and was clearly shocked. "Oops!" she said and then she saw the pillow which I threw on Sahil laying down and then she looked towards the bed and saw the crumpled sheets, she arched her eyebrow. I quickly picked it up and kept it on the bed. Damn it! Why had I not seen it before? Samar too had a horrified expression on his face seeing me. "Oh, I'm so sorry Sahil and Ananya, we did not know that you are here," Said Ridhima. "It's ok, we can wish him in the morning," Said Samar looking towards Sahil as he could sense out what was going on seeing the irritation on Sahil's face.

"No bhai, its ok, Ananya came to wish me and she was about to leave. It was cold outside so I gave my jacket to her. And bhai, you know I don't like cake cutting," Said Sahil seeing cake in Samar's hand. "Sahil we can cut the cake please," I said before he could say no again. I know he was irritated and so was I, we were about to take such a big step and were stopped in between. He quickly grabbed the knife from Ridhima's hand.

"Thank you bhaiya and Bhabhi," Said Sahil cutting the cake.

"Now we are going to leave you both," Said Samar smiling, "And Sahil button up your shirt properly. You have a lot of time now," He winked at Sahil making him blush like a teenager.

When they left Sahil exclaimed, "Shit! They knew what we were up to," He said scratching his head. "Ananya you could have stopped me." "I did try to stop you, but you were in no mood to listen." "Ananya, you were also enjoying everything. You kissed me back and hugged me tightly so I thought that even you want it," And he stopped himself. "Sahil you wanted to kiss me as your birthday gift."

"Even you were dying to kiss me Ananya."

"Oh, stop it Sahil. You are such a creep. Move, I need to go to the washroom." I removed Sahil's jacket as it was big enough for me and when I was about to wash my face I saw a dark red mark on my neck. Oh god! When did he do it ? "Sahil!" I shouted, "What the hell is this?"

He gave me his innocent look and asked, "What!?" I pointed towards my red mark. He grinned and said, "What! Grow up. It's a love bite." "I know it is a love bite, but why did you do it?"

"These things happen when we love each other."

"Ok, fine," I cut him in between as I didn't want to listen further. "When will this mark go and what am I suppose to do till then?" "I don't know and now stop irritating me Ananya and get out of my room And from next time don't wear these stupid Mickey Mouse dresses in my room." "Fine," I said and stormed out of his room. How can he be so rude!?

A minute ago he had loved me so tenderly and now he was behaving as if nothing happened. How could I lose myself into his arms thank god Samar came and brought me back to my senses? I thought he had changed, but no he is still the same arrogant and stubborn man, but I could feel so much love in his kiss. Zoya opened the door and looked towards me with dove eyes and said, "Ananya show me your return gift."

"Zoya, I'm your boss, you cannot question me, but thanks for supporting me."

"Seriously Ananya, you are such a baby. Wait a minute, what's there on your neck?" I tried to hide my gift with my hair, but it's impossible to hide a few things.

Zoya looked at my sullen face and fell on her bed laughing.

Chapter 22

In the morning at the breakfast table Samar announced that he had kept a birthday party for her daughter Reem and Sahil as it is their birthday today. Oh yes how could I forgot that Reem and Sahil shares the same birthday. Girls ran towards Sahil when they saw him coming downstairs and encircled him to wish him. He was looking dashing in his black and white striped shirt and black pant. He thanked them politely ignoring me. I did not felt like going to the party, but I wanted to meet Reem so half heartedly I got dressed wearing my off white colour dress which was slightly off shoulder as it was supported with thin strips of white flowers, but it was long this time, till my knees, and I was so comfortable wearing it. I applied light make up and left my hair open supported by a small clutch. I remember how Sahil used to love my long hair.

"Ananya you look so gorgeous, this white colour really suits you. Sahil sir will be dead seeing your charm today." "Zoya, we are getting late. I don't want to waste my time thinking about him." As we reached outside a taxi was waiting for us, Zoya smiled and said, "I already booked a taxi." We reached in five minutes as it was near-by.

It was a small place, the entrance was decorated beautifully with white and blue balloons, there was a cake in the centre of the room which was in the shape of a Mickey Mouse.

"See Zoya he ordered Mickey Mouse cake deliberately."

"Ananya, see how much he cares for you."

"Zoya you are mad for him, aren't you?"

"Yes Ananya, if he would have not been your love, I would have definitely tried my luck." "And Zoya, what about Vikram?" "Oh forget him now."

"No problem Zoya you can try your luck." She smiled and said, "He has his eyes only for you Ananya. I don't want to waste my time."

"Really Zoya so where are those eyes? And then I saw my handsome standing with Natasha wearing a navy blue colour sharp suit.

"Wow! Those eyes are on Natasha now. Have a look."

"They both look good together," Said Kavya placing her hand on my back. "Stop dreaming about him babes, he is moon for you."

I held Zoya's hand and said, Let's go from here."

"Ananya you look beautiful," Said Ridhima. She was wearing a light pink gown. I was not able to look her in her eyes. Zoya excused herself leaving us together. "Ananya we are so sorry about last night. Sahil must have been angry with you." "No, ma'am he was not," I knew Ridhima was right; he was behaving as if I was responsible for stopping him." "Come on Ananya, you can share it with me. It will be in between us, don't worry, girl talks." "Ok let me tell you one secret. Samar is also like this; he gets too irritated if he ever has to stop in between due to some reason. It just comes on their faces. I saw the same expression on Sahil's face yesterday." And she giggled.

"There was nothing going on ma'am." I said lowering my eyes down. "Ananya see I'm not interfering in your personal space, but its only you who can make him happy," And She brought my hair in front to cover the red mark. Oh God, how did my hair go back? I need to take care of this, idiot Sahil. I was so embarrassed to look at Ridhima.

"Hey, it's ok Ananya, we know how much you both love each other. It's just something that you both need to realize," and she took out a booby pin from her purse and inserted in my hair bringing, them in front, fixing them.

"Thanks Ridhima ma'am," she smiled and said, "Thanks to you Ananya, for bringing our Sahil back," and before leaving she said, "Ananya you can continue your left over task after the party is over," and she winked. They knew what was going on, this was so damn embarrassing!

Sahil did not even look at me once, and people think he loves me. Stupid Natasha was not leaving him and was he enjoying her. Finally, our wait was over when Reem entered the room along with Samar wearing a beautiful pink colour gown and she looked so beautiful. Sahil went and picked up Reem in his arms and kissed her on her cheeks. We all gathered around the cake. Sahil was standing in front of me; he glanced at me once and then turned the other side. Ridhima was right. He was irritated but why is he blaming me for that?

Reem looked so happy standing with Sahil, who encircled her in his arms and they both cut the cake together. I had not seen Sahil this happy in a long time. After the cake was cut, I took a small piece of cake and fed Reem, who looked at me with a not welcomed look, but she took a bite and the left over cream I rubbed on Sahil's face. I knew he will freak out, but this is what happens when you ignore me sweet heart. There was pin drop silence now. Samar's face was worth seeing which was full of panic. Ridhima's mouth was half open.

"What's wrong with you Ananya, when will you grow up? You know I hate all this stuff.

"What did you do, silly girl?" Said Natasha. Sahil was about to leave but I held his hand and said, "Let me clean it." "No, it's ok," and he jerked his hand away. "Instead of saying sorry you are behaving like this." I heard Samar saying, "let's enjoy the party guys." He knew I would handle him.

I liked Samar's confidence in me. "This is the cost you pay when you ignore me, Mr Sahil." He gave me a sharp look and said nothing. "I allowed you to kiss me and see the way you are behaving."

"You self invited yourself in my room and it was my wish."

"Right, kissing me without my permission." "Anaya you were into it too, savouring every moment. You forced me into it, that day also when I was drunk and you kissed me. You asked me to do it Ananya."

"Wow Sahil so smart of you, if I will ask you to kiss me now, will you do it?"

He smiled and said, "Why not? Try me." Thank god he smiled otherwise I would had died with guilt spoiling his birthday. "You are shameless and Ridhima saw the mark too."

"What!" Even he was embarrassed for a minute and then he grinned and said, "I will take care next time Ananya." He said and started moving.

"Shame less creature and where are you going? My love has come!" 'What' and when I turned I saw Reem standing in front of me, with a smile on her face, she ran and clung to Sahil.

I didn't want to budge in between, but was not able to stop myself. "Hi, Reem," I said but she faced the other side. "Aww just like your chachu," I said and he narrowed his eyes.

"Reem she is Ananya," said Sahil smiling. She looked at me and then at Sahil and said, "Your Ananya, chachu? Sahil looked at me guiltly and said, "Yes, my Ananya."

She ran towards me and hugged me taking Samar and Ridhima by surprise who also joined us. "Ananya di you are so beautiful. I always wished to meet you."

"And so did I. Can I come to meet you?" Asked Reem. "Of course Reem, I'm staying in your house only." "Wow," She said with excitement, "With chachu?" Making all of us go pale.

"No Reem not with your chachu. I'm staying in the guest house." "But why are you staying in the guest house?" She said innocently. "Reem let's go and eat the cake," Said Samar trying to handle the situation. "No," said Reem, "I will eat with my Chachu and Ananya di." She held my and Sahil's hand and dragged us to the cake.

She took a small plate and gave me a small bite and then to Sahil and then she ate herself. Everybody was shocked to see us bonding so well, there was smile on Sahil's and Reem's face. Spending time with Reem made me forget all my troubles and worry and I really enjoyed myself. Reem insisted upon me and Sahil to dance together and so here we were on the dance floor together dancing. Sahil's both hands were on my waist and he left no other option for me rather than to place, my hands on his shoulders and I knew he was enjoying it.

He came close and whispered in my ear, "Ananya where is my birthday gift I could sense mischief in his eyes?" "Why don't you ask for your gift from Natasha?" He looked in my eyes and smiled and said, "I will take it from her afterwards but she can't give me what you can."

I knew he was irritating me now. "I'm not kissing you any more Sahil, if you mean that.

He smiled and said, but we did not finish yesterday when bhai came in, I would like to finish it completely and he looked me in my eyes for an answer. Thank God he came otherwise god knows what had happened. "You loved it Ananya, didn't you?" I pushed him a little and said, "It won't happen again, jerk," and left him smiling on the dance floor. Thank God Reem was not there waiting for us. I was standing with Zoya with a drink and Sahil and Samar were standing together, but his eyes were all on me,

"See Ananya I told you he will not be able to take his eyes from you, and look at Natasha and Kavya they both are sulking in the corner."

"Hi Ananya!" Somebody tapped me on my shoulder, I looked behind and before I could react Ritvik picked me up in his arms, swayed me around and kissed me on my cheeks.

"Ritvik, put me down." I could feel all the eyes on me. "Hey Ananya, come on we met after such a long time. Didn't you miss me?" "I missed you Ritvik but…"

"Ananya you are lying. You did not miss me; you did not even call me in so many days."

"Oh I'm so sorry Ritvik. How have you been.? "Bored without you, Ananya."

I saw Manoj coming towards us. I looked towards Sahil and Samar and they both were standing lifeless like a statue. "Hey Ritvik!" Said Manoj, "Good to see you. Now you can take care of Ananya. She had been acting weird from sometime." "Really?" Said Ritvik engulfing me in an arm, smiling. "By the way it is Mr. Sahil's birthday today. So kindly wish him," Told Manoj.

"Yes, I'm going to wish him," and before I could tell him anything, he dragged me towards Sahil and Samar. Ritvik was still holding my hand. I saw Sahil's blood boiling in his eyes.

He held out his hand to wish Sahil and said, "happy birthday bhai." I looked at Ritvik. But my Mr. Angry was in no mood to answer. "Who invited you to this party?"

"I just came to wish you."

"I don't need your wishes. Please leave."

"Chill bro, I came to meet my friend Ananya. Manoj told me she is here." Sahil looked at me and then at Ritvik and said, "You can take her and get lost from here." And he turned the other side. "Bhai have you forgotten all your manners? Don't insult Ananya."

"I can do what I wish Ritvik. I can talk to her the way I want. You don't teach me."

"When will you learn to talk nicely to women, bhai." "Ritvik please," I tried to stop him but he did not listen. Samar came towards us and said, "Ananya please leave before it is too late."

"Ritvik please for God's sake, you are a mature person and it's his birthday."

"Yeah, right, Miss Ananya," said Sahil. "He is a mature person; so take your mature person from here who is not invited in the party." He said a little too loud for everyone to see. There was a crowd surrounding us by now.

Ridhima came running towards us and said, "Sahil there is a phone call for you."

"I don't want to talk to anybody bhabhi." "It's Niya on line she wants to wish you as your phone is not reachable." Niya, my best friend! She was still in touch with Sahil? How could she be in touch with him and not with me? Sahil saw me looking at him and he took the phone from Ridhima and went away.

"Let's go Ananya," said Ritvik and dragged me out of the party. I made Ritvik stop half way.

I wanted to tell him about Sahil, but what's the use dragging the past, but if he got to know about me kissing Sahil from somebody he will be upset. "Ritvik, first you tell me how you know Sahil?" I asked him. He looked at me and said in a mellow voice, "He is my half brother."

I was shocked to hear this. Ritvik was Sahil's brother that's why he resembles so much to him. "Ananya my mother married my father as they both were in love and so Sahil and I are not on talking terms, as Sahil always insults my mother and blamed her for leaving him and his father. I knew Sahil is good at heart, but he always insulted my mother and so we both don't share a good repo. Samar does not take more interest as he had always stayed out, so he is not so attached with mumma, but my mother is my life and I tried a lot to cope with Sahil's tantrum and bad nature and see he suffers so much, his wife left him, he is the same like his father drunkard man who does not know how to respect women."

Ritvik got scared seeing me crying, "I'm sorry because of me you have to leave this party." "It's not that Ritvik," I said weeping." T"hen why are you crying?" "It's about Sahil," I said wiping my tears. He came close to me and held my shoulder with his hands and said, "Why Ananya did he said something to you or did he insult you? I know he is good at it."

"No, no, Ritvik just stop being so negative about him." Ritvik looked towards me with his big shocked eyes. "He is not so bad, but the circumstances made him like this and you yourself said this to me once." "I can't believe you Ananya; you are taking his side, as if you know him."

I lowered my eyes and said, "yes, I know him very closely Ritvik. He was my boyfriend and I loved him like mad and I knew this that he missed his mother so much."

Ritvik was shocked, expressionless. "It was Sahil who left you heartbroken? He ruined your life and still you are favouring him?"

"I did not know the reason then."

"And he is a kid at his heart, an egoistic stubborn baby and you are much more mature then him though you are his younger brother. And you also know this, that his life is hell and he is going through a roller coaster and he had no one to love him back. He is alone Ritvik no one standing with him. Samar is busy with his family and work, you had your mom with you if you ever felt lonely and your friends and your girlfriend and look at him, he is a loner he doesn't have anybody with him. His wife left him, his daughter whom he loves like manic is not there with him, he doesn't have friends like you. Just think about it Ritvik, you are a psychiatrist and you can comprehend with him more, don't look at him as your brother but as one of your patients." Ritvik looked at me and asked me, "Have you forgiven him?"

"No, I want to forgive him, but I'm not able to forget the time which I spent crying for him, but one thing I know Ritvik, that he needs lots of love." "I know but I'm feeling sad not because you are his love interest because

I know, he loves you to insanity and he will not like if you will talk to me, but I'm happy that he has fallen in love with a girl like you ,who had a golden heart so pure and not filled with malice like other girls. Don't get me wrong Ananya but things are not well between us and I think I created more rifts between you two now." "There is nothing between us now. I don't think I can think of being in relation with him. We both have come a long way without each other and in a few days, I will be going back to Delhi and he will be here."

"Ananya you can give a second chance to him. I know I don't like Sahil much ,but I still care for him and I want him to be settled in his life and I'm dam sure you can mend relation between this mother and son and, he will definitely help you in the kitchen, he is a very good cook."

"Ritvik now you are being naughty."

"It's ok bhabhi, no problem."

"Omg! Stop calling me bhabhi."

We laughed now and then we saw Sahil coming out in anger with a bottle of whiskey in his hands. He gave a dirty look to us and thrashed the bottle on the ground near us. And in a second he sat in his car and drove off speedily. Samar and Ridhimaa came out running after him. "What happened? Is he alright?" Samar ignored my question and came towards Ritvik. "Ritvik you knew it was his birthday, he was celebrating his birthday after so many years and you ruined it." "Samar bhaiya he just came to meet me." "Ananya I'm so upset with you, if you were dating Ritvik why you did not maintain your distance with Sahil?

"He had started changing in your company.

"Did you do this deliberately to hurt him?" "Samar bhaiya..." Ritvik tried to intervene, but he was shown

Samar's hand and he was in a bad temper. But it was enough for me now, and I had to shout on top of my voice, "Samar bhaiya please listen to me. Ritvik is not my boyfriend; he just came to see me because we are friends and secondly Ritvik has a girlfriend."

Samar was quiet for a moment. I was so worried about Sahil; I knew he must have been upset. Everybody's mood was spoiled and so we returned back without eating anything.

"I 'am so sorry Ananya," said Ritvik before leaving. I sat with a thud on the bed, keeping my hand on my head ,my past is haunting me now ,everybody whom I left five years back are coming back to me. Sahil and now Niya, Where must she be? But right now I was worried about Sahil. I had asked Samar bhiya to call me or text me once he's back.

"Ananya don't worry. Sahil sir will come."

"I don't know Zoya when will he grow up."

She giggled a little.

"You know Ananya, you both are so cute, Sahil sir was saying the same thing to me for you yesterday, when will she grow up wearing Mickey mouse dresses, and one more thing Ananya, Sahil booked the taxi for us and said I don't want her to go alone so I'm sending my friend's car to fetch you both." "What? Why you did not tell me?" "Because Sahil sir said not to tell you otherwise you will not sit in the car. See Ananya I told you he cares for you a lot."

It was 2 in the morning now and there was no message from Samar bhiya.

I thought of calling him, but somehow managed to stop myself.

I closed my eyes for a second and I heard a beep, It was a text from Samar bhiya.

'Ananya he is back and he is drunk like hell, One of his friends came to leave him and he is sleeping now.'

Thank god he was back, but why did he start drinking so much even after knowing it destroyed his father's life? I woke up feeling tired as I had slept little during the night. Zoya was ready for breakfast, so I quickly brushed my teeth and got ready changing from my Mickey Mouse night suit into a pair of jeans.

"Ananya you are so fond of your jeans," Had said Sahil when he had come to take me for dinner that day, our equation had changed overnight then and now the tables are reversed. Am I the reason of his misery, I was feeling sad for ruining his birthday.

I remembered Niya's call yesterday on Sahil's birthday; how come she is in touch with Sahil? She was not so fond of him. I can't even ask him now; I knew he will not talk to me, my hot headed egoistic Sahil. There was no sign of him at the table and only Samar was eating his breakfast, his head bowed. I asked Zoya to excuse me for a second and made my way to Samar. I don't care anymore about the other people sitting there and was in a no mood to listen to stupid sarcastic comments of Natasha. Samar gave me his meek smile and asked me to sit and placed a plate in front of me, but I pushed it away.

All I could ask him was is he awake, I was feeling so guilty about the whole situation yesterday. "Samar bhaiya I'm so sorry for all that happened yesterday, but it was not done intentionally."

"I know Ananya you are not lying, but you know Sahil how he is it took a long time for him to come out of his cocoon just because of you and now again he is so distinct and aloof like the old Sahil." Samar again pushed the plate towards me and said, "Ananya eat something, he will be ok it's the hangover," and then we saw Sahil coming downstairs with one hand on his head and still wearing clothes from last night. He came and sat in front of me and said, "Bhaiya from when did you started entertaining employees on our family table?" Samar began to reply but I signalled him not to. It was stupidity talking to him with his sour mood.

So I stood up and went to the other table and sat down and saw Natasha and Kavya laughing.

"How many boyfriends do you have Ananya?" asked Natasha grinning. "Two or three," said Kavya, "She looked so innocent just engrossed in her work, but see how see is, her real face is out now. She wants to trap all our handsome managers," Both giggled. .

"Enough is enough Natasha," I yelled making everybody look at me, even Sahil and Samar. "Don't you dare cross your limits?" "Oh really Ananya just because I told the truth that you are sleeping around with different high profile man?" Natasha had crossed all her limits now and I did not cared about the consequences now and stood up and gave her a tight slap and said, "Shut up you dirty minded witch, I'm not like you." Everybody was shocked. Nobody had seen me this angry. Without eating my breakfast, I went straight away to my room and started crying. Why are you doing this with me Sahil, why are you treating me like this?

Ritvik is not my boyfriend, and if he was also then what was the big deal , we are no longer together ,then why does this bother you? We can't we be together ever now Sahil?

I don't want to be heartbroken again, I don't have enough strength now. I heard a knock on the door and opened it to see Zoya with a sad face. "Are you ok? You know Natasha created so much tamasha there on the table crying."

"Did Sahil say anything?" " No, but he did not have his breakfast and went upstairs after you left. Samar tried to stop him, but he said I am not feeling well." Tears came down running my eyes.

"Samar scolded Natasha and said such personal comments will not be entertained in my house."

I hugged Zoya and said, "I'm not worried about all this, what I'm worried about is Sahil has not eaten anything since last night."

"And neither have you. What kind of people are you both? You both are madly in love with each other, if one is not eating the other person doesn't eat! Why don't you confront him with your feeling and clear all the misunderstanding, Ananya?"

"No, Zoya, I love him and I will always love him, but there is no future together as my parents will never be ready for this relation now as they have seen me suffering so much.

My mother just hates Sahil and always blames him for ruining my life." "You can make them understand Ananya; they will figure it out slowly. Zoya, seeing me heartbroken and not yet married they had become so depressed and if I will marry Sahil, they will stop talking to me and I don't know what will they do to themselves? I can't be so selfish. I will choose my parents over my love now." Zoya held my hands and said, "What will you do with some other man whom you can't love? Ananya you can give a try don't lose hope, there is still time."

Chapter 23

I needed some fresh air to clear my mind so I just went outside to take a walk. After walking for a while a bright light fell on me from back as there was a car behind my back and the driver was desperate to gain my attention. I turned back irritated to smash the person sitting in the car with my harsh words, but all my anger vanish when I saw Ritvik driving coming out of the car. "Hey Ananya how are you?"

"Hey Ritvik, what are you doing here?"

"I was coming to meet you and see I got lucky," and he gave me his beautiful carefree smile. I wished If Sahil was also like him. "All well Ananya?" He got worried seeing my ashen face.

"Ya just a bit tired."

"Ok , so lets go for a short drive."

"No Ritvik may be some other time."

"Ananya, you know I won't budge so please sit in the car."

You sounded like your big brother, but I agreed as I knew that a drive was, much needed to let me forget everything running in my mind.

"So how is the angry man?" I smiled and asked "Still angry?" Ritvik laughed and said, "Strange, he is still angry. I know he must have not given you a chance to speak."

"Wow Ritvik you know quite a lot about him." His expression changed into gloomy one.

"He doesn't consider me his brother, but I know my brother very well. Mom is always talking about him. I wish Sahil could mellow down a bit and forget about the past."

"He surely will one day when his life is more sorted," I quipped.

"Only you can do this, Ananya. I don't understand how he could let you go away from his life like this and why is he not doing anything to get you back in his life. I have seen him suffering for you. He used to look pathetic before his marriage days and anybody could make out from his face on the wedding day that he was being forced into this marriage. He was completely heartbroken. Even I was really upset for him.

Ananya I know that circumstances were against him but when he insults my mother I feel like breaking his bones," And then he stopped looking towards me. "I'm sorry Ananya. I don't mean to hurt you."

"He doesn't hate your mother, but it's the pain which he had gone through without her. It's the pain of the loneliness he went through, it's the pain of craving the love from his mother when he wanted. He missed her so much and that loss comes out in the form of hatred."

Ritvik looked into my eyes as if searching for something. "Ananya you understand him so well and see being a doctor I was not able to relate my feeling and you had given it the exact words. Do you want to take away my position? I'm scared." And we both laughed.

"This is because you are looking at him as your brother and not like your patient."

"You know when I saw you for the first time you made me think of Sahil. You both look so similar," Said Ananya.

He gave a blushing nod and replied, "It is because we both share similar features as my mother."

After a long refreshing drive Ritvik dropped me outside the guesthouse.

"Take care Ananya bhabhi and sweet dreams of my brother."

"Ha...ha...Ritvik don't be naughty."

As I was about to enter the gate, I saw Sahil coming out of the gate. He looked towards me and then to the car from which I had stepped out and then looked in his watch and passed me banging the gate loudly. "Uh...oh...Why is he here at this time and being so overdramatic, jealous freak? I went up to my room and changed and lay down on the bed.

The next week in the office was quite hectic as the submission of the reports were close and the company had started working on new ways and techniques to improve the profit earning capacity of the company, and the result had been quiet positive. Company had started making profits now, with some additional benefits to the employees there were less employees leaving the company.

We all were so engrossed in our works that time went unnoticed. It looked like Sahil and I had completely jumped into work. We hardly talked to each other about anything other than work. In a way it was better that we were so engrossed in our works and it would not be difficult for me to go from here in next 10 days.

Sahil was not talking to me after that incident and even I did not try to talk to him, but I really wanted to know about Niya and Karan. So one day at office, I asked him, "Are you in touch with Niya?" He looked at me for a second but did not answer. "Sahil I'm asking you something." It's not your concern anymore Miss Ananya."

"God damn it Sahil! She is my friend."

"She was your friend but now she is my friend."

"Sahil please," I said almost teary eyed, "Why are you behaving with me like this? I will be leaving Delhi in the next 10 days. Please show some humanity." He was quiet for a moment and then said, "She is in London working with a firm."

"Is she married?"

"Yeah they both got married last year."

"They both means?"

"Ananya stop behaving as if you don't know about Niya and Karan.

"All I knew was Karan and Niya broke up long back and then I lost touch with Niya."

"Yes they broke up, but they were meant for each other. They were back with each other after one year and now they are married and living happily." Tears were in my eyes now, "Wow! I'm so happy for them. Can you give me their numbers?

But you and Niya did not get along well and she stopped talking to you when you left me," finally I said it.

"I will text you the number. You can talk to her and stop disturbing me with your girly talk." "You know what Sahil you are impossible to talk with."

"I'm not your boyfriend Ananya. Go and tell this to your mature boyfriend Ritvik."

"He is not my boy friend Sahil and he already has a girlfriend whom he is about to marry, but I wished that he was my boyfriend because he is not like you at all. He doesn't insult me all the time and neither is he so insensitive like you." I shouted at the top of my voice. "Sahil you left me five years back ruining my life, and see how you are behaving with me every day as if I left you like this, as if I am responsible for ruining your life."

"For a while I thought that we could start our relation afresh, when I knew that you were forced to marry that women, but now I regret thinking that way for you. You have really changed and I can feel that there is no place left in your heart for me. It would be a wise decision that we stay away from each other."

He stood up and said, "You are right. We were not meant for each other," and he moved out of his room leaving me crying.

He had changed so much. I should not be crying for this heartless man. My Sahil would have never left me crying like this. He does not love me anymore, I realised and I wiped my tears.

I wanted to call Niya that very moment, but decided to wait till I reach home from office so that I can talk to her in peace. After taking my dinner, I went for a stroll in the garden so that I could talk to Niya. I needed to ask so many things to her and didn't want to get disturbed by anybody.

I dialled Niya's number crossing my fingers. The phone was picked up after three rings and a male voice answered the call, "Hello, who is this?" It did not take me a second to recognize that it was Karan on the line. "Hello, who is this? He said again, but I was unable to speak, as if the words were choking in my throat. After a few seconds all I could utter was, "Karan" in my sobbing voice. There was silence on the phone for a second and then he said, "Anu".

"Hmm its me."

"Oh my God!" he shouted like anything, "Niya come quick! It is Anu on the line."

"Anu! Where were you for so many years? We tried so hard to find you. You were not on any social media sites and there was no information about you."

"Karan you stopped talking to me." He was silent now and said, "I know Anu, circumstances were such. You know it was difficult for me to tell you things about Sahil. You both were in so much pain, it was tough for me to see you both like this. I felt so helpless. The best I could do was distance myself from you. I am sorry. Sahil was working with me and I know I can't lie to you any further. That's why I stopped talking to you, but after sometime I tried a lot to trace you, but was not able to. Anu I'm so sorry, but how did you get Niya's number? She missed you a lot too."

I was crying now..and I knew Karan too was. "Hey, stop crying. I wish I was there with you. I would have hugged you so tight, you wouldn't have been able to shed another tear."

"Me too Karan. I missed you both so much."

"Who is it Karan?" I heard a voice from behind."

"Its Anu!"

"Anu! Oh God and she started crying, "Where were you my baby? It's been so long, you changed your number and did not bother to SMS me again. I missed you so much. Where were you and how did you get my number?"

"I got it from Sahil. I heard him talking to you on his birthday."

"Oh Sahil? Are you in touch with him?"

"Yaa. I'm In Bangalore and working along with him on the same project but I would be leaving Bangalore in the next 10 days."

"Ohh Ananya are you both...,"

"No Niya." I did not let her finish her sentence. "Sahil is a changed man now. He is more arrogant and more cold hearted than ever. He is not my Sahil whom I loved and I cannot forgive him for inflicting me with so much pain. But how are you in touch with him?"

"Anu you know today Karan and I are together just because of him. He sorted out the differences between us and he convinced my parents for our marriage. They were completely against it. You are saying that he has changed a lot but we have seen him go through a lot. Look, I'm not saying that you did not suffer, but Sahil blame himself each day for leaving you like this. When he got divorced, I asked him to search for you, but he was reluctant and said I ruined her life and I should be punished for it.

I tried to look for you too but you changed your number. I even called your home but your mom picked up the phone and said don't call my daughter again."

"Yaa, I told her not to give my number as I wanted to get away from that life. but I have missed you so much and when I heard that you were on the phone that day with Sahil, I could not resist talking to you."

"Thankyou, Ananya you called me. I can't tell you how happy I'm talking to you, and how dare Sahil did not tell us about you. We are coming there next week and I will pull his ears when I come there. Is he behaving ok with you now?"

I was quite. "Tell me if you still consider me your friend," I started crying again, "No Niya he does not leave a stone unturned to annoy me. He has become so cold hearted but please don't say anything to him. I don't want him back in my life, its ok for me now." "Anu I know you still love him, don't you?"

"No, I don't and let's not talk about him. I'm so happy you are coming to India and I can meet you before going."

"Me too."

Talking to Niya was like fresh blood infused into my body and I was happy that she was coming to India and that now I will always be in touch with her. I know how much I missed her in my life. They both were my life support. I turned around wiping my tears and there he was standing like a statue with hands behind his back. He made me scream. "Oh gosh Sahil! you scared me. What the hell are you doing here?"

"Listening to your conversation. How dare you Sahil? Better mind your own business." "Ananya have you seen the time? It's 11 at night. I saw you roaming in the garden alone from my window. When will you learn to be careful? You know the gates are not closed and that stupid boy Kunal who mixed alcohol is still staying here, due to your mercy. How do you take care of yourself in Delhi alone?"

"Sahil it is your problem that you think I'm a baby."

"Yeah, I know. Now please come and I will leave you to your room. I'm feeling sleepy."

There was no light from the garden to my room and I thought he is so right, how could I be so stupid. "Ok," I said to him, "Now that you have come here, you can walk with me till my room but not beyond that." Sahil gave me a stare and said, "I don't go anywhere where I'm not invited."

"Fine, let's go now. I don't want to fight with you."

"So what did Niya say? She must be happy."

"Yaa, she was and I told her how you behave with me and she said she will come here and pull your ears."

"Ananya this is ridiculous. When will you grow up? Stop being a cry baby."

"Ohh wow, look at yourself first."

"What do I look at? I know I'm good enough."

"Yaa, yaa, you are good enough at hurting and you don't eve spare your mother." I regretted saying this immediately."

"And who told you this crap, your boy friend?"

"Sahil I told you he is not my boyfriend and he is your brother."

"Ananya don't call him my brother! He is not."

"Why are you so negative about him? Ritvik is a nice guy."

"He may be nice to you, but not for me."

"Sahil you force him to behave like this. When will you move on from your past, why can't you forgive Ritvik and your mother? She was in love." Hearing this, Sahil lost his control, and grabbed my hand tightly.

"Please leave my hand, you are hurting me."

"You have crossed all your limits today."

"Please, what is wrong with you? Leave my hand."

"Now you are spending so much time with Ritvik that he is telling you that my mother was right. So tell me Ananya what else did he tell you? Did he took you to his house and make you happy enough to forget me?"

This was enough for me. I slapped him hard across his face. I had not dreamt of doing this in my life, but how could he talk nonsense about me, when he knows me so well. "How dare you Sahil?" I said with angry tears. "Just go away from my life. I hate you. Just get lost and don't show me your face. You are a coward Sahil and you always will be one."

"YES! he shouted, "I'm a coward. Why don't you go and marry your boyfriend then?"

Zoya came out hearing the commotion. One look at us and she was perplexed. "What's going on here?"

"Zoya, just ask this man to leave." Sahil was standing with his hand on his cheek, unable to accept the pain or the insult I guess. I came inside and slammed the door on his face.

I hugged Zoya and cried hard. "Mam what happened? What did Sahil sir said to you?" But I could only cry. "Zoya I want to leave this place as soon as possible. I can't take this bullshit again. I will resign tomorrow if they don't let me go from here tomorrow. I am devastated by the man whom I loved like hell. Today he crossed all his limits and I will not forgive him for what he said today."

"Please calm down and try to sleep. We will talk about this in the morning." Zoya cajoled.

I cried the whole night and cursed myself for loving him and wondering how could he say such offensive things to me?

Chapter 24

I woke up in the morning and got ready and went directly to the office early without taking Zoya along with me. I knew Manoj comes early in the office so I went to his cabin and luckily he was there, "May I come in?" He looked up. "Ananya, what happened? Are you all right?" "Ya Manoj I'm but my mother is not well," and I lied to run from the situation. "But Ananya only few days are left and how can you go now?"

"Manoj please all the reports are made, implementation is also done and company had started making a profit, what else do you want?"

"I know, but still they need us for last minute if there is any kind of loophole."

"Manoj please I'm requesting you, my mother is not well and if you will not give me the permission, unfortunately I will resign right now."

Manoj was shocked.

"Ananya is your mother so serious? I know you had never asked for leave; ok give me one day's time, I need to discuss this with Samar."

"No, Manoj please, you are my manager. I need your permission, not his."

"You are reporting to Samar so you have to take his permission."

"Then ask him right now."

"What is wrong with you? Ok, you go and sit in Sahil's cabin and I will be back."

"No," I shouted, "I will not sit with that moron." Manoj looked at me in disbelief.

"Is he the problem Ananya?"

"No Manoj please I don't want to go and sit there. I'm ok here. "

Manoj stood up and went outside in panic. I was so hurt that I did not feel like doing anything. Only Sahil had the power to break me like this always. Everybody says he had suffered a lot, but nobody cares how much he always makes me suffer.

I was startled by the phone call in Manoj's cabin. I picked up and it was Manoj.

"Ananya can you please come in Sahil's cabin?"

"I'm not coming there!"

"Please. Samar is also here. You need to come here please," and he disconnected the line

Shit! I would have to face him again. But why am I afraid, he should be feeling sorry for talking bullshit to me. I entered Sahil's cabin and all the three heads turned towards me.

"Ananya, what is wrong with you?" freaked Samar, "How can you go without completing your work?" I felt hurt as Samar did not notice my puffy eyes; he was only concerned about his work. But soon he noticed, "What happened? Are you not well?" He asked, concerned.

Sahil was not even looking at me. "My mother is not well Samar, that's why I want to go."

"Really?" asked Sahil and the next moment he took out his cell phone and dialled a number on loud speaker. No! He still had her number and my mother was quick to respond too. Damn it! Why am I always caught if I ever try to lie? "Hello," said my mother. "Hello aunty," replied Sahil. "I'm calling from Ananya's office at Bangalore."

"Why, what happened? Is Ananya all right?"

"Yes, don't worry. She is all right," and he brought the phone to me to speak with her, on loudspeaker. "Mumma don't worry I'm ok, my phone was not working and so I called from my colleague's phone." "Thank God beta, you are ok. Ananya me and your father are going to attend a function nearby, I will talk to you later bacha." "Ok mom, take care."

"And Ananya listen, I have seen a nice boy for you."

"Mumma, please stop it, we can talk later" I saw anger in Sahil's eyes.

"So, you were lying," Said Manoj.

"Why do you pretend when you can't lie Miss. Ananya?" Remarked Sahil.

"I'm not talking to you Mr. Sahil and I'm not answerable to you as you are not my boss, so please stop irritating me."

"Ananya, I thought that for you professionalism is your priority," said Samar scowling.

"It is my priority sir. I have always placed my work before everything, but I'm also a human. I also get hurt if somebody tries to hurt me again and again.

I looked at Manoj and said, "I want to resign, if you will not allow me to go."

Sahil banged his hand on the table and shouted, "Bhai why are you tolerating her and why don't you let her go? I can manage without her."

"I know you can manage without me Sahil like always."

"Just stop it both of you!" Shouted Samar.

"Manoj can you please leave us alone for some time?" Manoj frowned, but moved out of the cabin. Samar stood up and latched the door from inside. "What is wrong with the both of you?"

Samar came towards me and kept his hand on my shoulder and said, "Ananya tell me the truth. Did he say something to you?"

"Bhai please, again, you are asking her?"

"Sahil I'm talking to Ananya. Please don't interfere between us."

My mouth was devoid of words. I just started crying.

"Hey Ananya, stop crying and tell me what did he do to you?"

I just said, "Please Samar bhaiya, I want to go from here."

"Ananya I know you are a strong woman and you can't leave like this just because some people don't trust you," And he gave a cold stare to Sahil.

"If a person doesn't care for you it is his loss, you should care a damn for that person."

Sahil stood up and walked out of the cabin, banging the door.

He continued, "I know Sahil has hurt you, and I don't know why is he doing this, but you should not cry for him, if he doesn't understand you. I'm not saying this to hold you back for work, but I know my brother is a fool if he will let you go away from his life."

"I don't want him in my life," I said crying some more.

"So, don't let him win. This time if you left, you will not go like this just because of Sahil, and it is not an order from your boss. If you ever consider me your bhaiya which you always call me, so think that your brother is requesting you to stay back. Can you do this for your brother? Please Ananya for our sake." I looked at him and smiled and said, "Ok bhaiya, just for you."

I wish Ritvik was here with me, but he was out on a vacation with Priya and I didn't want to spoil it for him. I was just counting my days now.

I started sitting in Samar's cabin and made it a point not to come in front of Sahil and Samar also took care of this.

Finally the day was there and we were called for the meeting.

Mr. Subarmaniyam thanked all of us for our hard work and dedication which in turn helped his company to come out of the slump and garner profits.

"I want to thank every employee for putting in their hard work from top managers to trainee who worked day and night to help our company to come in this position and we will all miss you, so let's get together for a small farewell party which is organized in my bungalow. It's an order that everybody will be present there and everybody started laughing and you can also bring along your friends in our party. The details about the party will be on the board."

Everybody was gathered around the board like a bee to collect information.

The theme was traditional.

"Ananya do you know how to wear a Saree?" "Yes, don't worry I'll help you."

"But I don't have a saree. Let's go and buy one."

"Zoya please you go. I'm not coming to that party."

"Why? Please. You have come a long way, please don't do this. And sir, will feel offended if you will not go," But there was a lump in my throat. I didn't want to go, but my heart wanted to see Sahil for the last time. I know I hated him for what he said to me few days back, but my heart knew that I was still in love with him and this time I wanted to see him properly before leaving.

"Ok. I will come to the party, but please don't force me to go shopping."

"Ok, you can rest, but what will you wear?

"I have a saree."

"Ok then I will go directly from here and you get ready, then only you can get me ready." "Yeah sure," I came back to my room and took out a beautiful pink saree from my cupboard. I layed down and closed my eyes. "Ananya, I brought a gift for you."

"Wow Sahil, what is it?"

"Just look at it yourself," I quickly tore open the bag and saw a beautiful pink saree. "Wow, it is lovely Sahil, thank you so much." He pulled me towards him and kissed me on my forehead and said, "One day I would love to see you wearing this saree only for me and then we can dance together."

He brought tears to my eyes that day as we kissed. There were tears in my eyes again and I said to myself that day has come Sahil. I will wear this saree only for you today. I hope you remember it.

I got ready by 5 with a light make up and my long traces flowing down just like he used to like it. I wanted to live each moment now as I knew that it would be the last day for the both of us to see each other.

Zoya came rushing in breaking my reverie. "Sorry, I'm late," she was surprised to see the way I was looking. She slowly said, "You look so mesmerising in this saree."

Zoya had bought a light blue saree which was looking beautiful on her and soon we were ready to go out to the party. Subramanian sir had kept the party at his farm house, and he had managed to arrange a bus for us to his house for our safety.

Natasha and Kavya weren't happy looking at me but I was least bothered and wanted to enjoy the party.

We reached in 20 minutes; his farm house was really grand and the ambience was awesome, decorated with flowers and light everywhere There was a swimming pool too which was surrounded by tables and chairs to sit and there were lights on every tree and balloons tied up on the trees. It was looking magnificent. "Wow! sir has spent a lot of money on this because he has started making lots of money again," I said and winked at Zoya.

There were drinks and snacks outside and the food and dance floor was inside the house.

Soon we all were gathered inside the big house for the cake cutting.

I spotted Samar along with Ridhima.

"Hey Ananya," said Ridhima, "You look so beautiful."

"So do you ma'am. I was looking for Sahil here and there now. Ridhima noticed and said "Ananya he is there, right behind you." I at once looked back and he was looking at me. When he saw I was looking at him, he turned his gaze the other way as usual. He was looking dashing in his black suit.

"Ananya I don't understand you both are not able to take your eyes off each other and I have seen you handling him so well and it's only you he allows him to dominate as he doesn't listen to anybody else. What is stopping you both? You both are made for each other."

"Ridhima ma'am sometimes what is seen is not the truth." and saying this I excused myself from there." I wanted to hide in one corner and just keep looking at Sahil for one last time. I know he had hurt me, but still somewhere in my heart I longed to be with him. If he had asked me out again, maybe I have said yes, but he looks so distant and aloof from me now. When he kissed me that day there was so much love that I had felt. I had thought that he still feels for me, but now he was a changed man as if he doesn't care anymore. Soon we all were circled around the big cake.

Subramanian sir stood in front of us. My Sahil was standing behind him eyeing me carefully. Can't he get the guts to come in front of me and look at me properly?

Coward! I averted my gaze too. The cake was cut and Mr. Subramanian was the happiest man on the earth. "The dance floor is open now!" He shouted. "Enjoy guys and thank you all for the support and coming and joining me in this evening."

Everybody was dancing like a manic as if their own company has earned profit, eating and drinking gleefully

I was standing with Zoya, but my eyes were on Sahil, who was also giving me hidden glances.

"Why don't you just go and talk to him?"

"I don't need to talk to him anymore Zoya."

"Then why are you staring at him? You both do not stop looking at each other."

She was quiet for a few minutes.

"Ananya, you are making the biggest mistake of your life. You will not be happy without him. How will you live without him.?"

"Hey gorgeous!" Ritvik was standing in front of me.

I saw Sahil moving away from my gaze and the reason was evident.

But I didn't care anymore. "Thanks Ritvik, but it wasn't my choice." I replied to his appreciative eye.

"It's your elder brother's choice."

Zoya and Ritvik both gave me a look. "Woooh!" said Zoya, "Sir gifted you this Saree!"

"Yaa, he did, but five years back," Zoya and Ritvik's surprise was evident on their faces.

"Are you kidding me Ananya?" said Ritvik, "You guys are so obsessed with each other. Is he still angry at you? "Yeah, he is, and looking at you he must be burning now."

"How can my elder brother be jealous of me? Tell him that I have a girlfriend."

"He is so stupid letting you go Ananya, he should be lucky that god is giving him a second chance, only you could made him a good human."

"Ritvik he is a good human just a bit angry."

"When you know all this Ananya why don't you approach him?"

I didn't want to tell Ritvik what Sahil said to me, "I know that it would ensue a fight."

"But if he feels like this, let him feel it."

"Leave it Ritvik, just tell me how was your vacation with Priya?"

"Oh, it was great," and he blushed.

"Wow Ritvik, really I'm so happy for you.

"Can we dance?" He gave me an odd look.

"Do you want to make my brother jealous?"

"Yes I want to, come," and I dragged him on the dance floor.

A soft track was playing for the couple to dance together.

Ritvik and I danced like any other couple and all eyes were on us, I could feel his eyes also.

Good get jealous now, if you think this way that I'm having an affair with Ritvik ,so now you look how I behave.

"Can I dance with the lady now?" A firm voice stopped us.

Ritvik looked at him and I shrieked and leaving Ritvik's hand hugged the beholder of the new voice tightly.

Karan and I cried like a baby. Everybody was shocked to see me hugging him and I could feel Kavya and Natasha dying with jealousy. Ritvik was also confused seeing Karan, who wiped my tears from my face and kissed me on my head and said, "Where were you Anu? I and Niya missed you so much." I recalled my manners and introduced the guys, "Ritvik, he is Karan my best friend. And this is Ritvik." "Yes, I know him, he is Sahil's brother, but what is he doing with you."

"I'm dancing with Ananya," Ritvik was quick to answer, "because my elder brother does not value his love for this lady anymore."

Karan looked at me and then towards Sahil, who was staring at us all, standing along with Niya.

I could not control myself now and seeing her I left Karan and ran to greet Niya and so did she, and we both hugged each other for a really long time and cried.

"Anu how have you been? You look even more beautiful, and with whom are you dancing? You should be dancing with Sahil."

"Niya please Sahil is no more interested in me and he is Ritvik my friend and Sahil's younger half-brother."

"Oh, that's why he was giving a cold stare looking towards both of you dancing and when I asked him who is Ananya dancing with and he said, her charming mature boyfriend."

"He has gone out of his mind Niya. He is not my boyfriend and Sahil is not able to believe this."

"Ananya, you were about to dance with me", said Karan and drag me to the dance floor.

"Oh, yes come let's dance. Niya you can dance with the angry man standing there," said Karan signalled towards Sahil, who was feeling most neglected now.

Karan took me to the dance floor and Niya dragged Sahil on the dance floor.

"How come you both are here?"

"Samar invited us, when he came to know that we were coming to India, and we both want to surprise you both."

"I loved the surprise, but how cum Niya brought Sahil on the dance floor so easily." I asked Karan.

"Oh, they both share a great rapport now. Sahil consider Niya as her sister, and he comes to us every year on Rakhi, and their bond is inseparable. He obeys her now and Niya can often fight with me to save her brother."

"Wow, that's sounds great. Ananya you know he was so broken, have you forgiven him Ananya?"

"Karan he seemed to be a changed man now, he is not that Sahil whom I loved."

"He did not once say that he is sorry for leaving me, rather he is always irritating and insulted me." I didn't want to tell Karan what he had said to me, I know he would have also not tolerated.

"Should I talk to him Ananya?"

"No Karan he is big enough to take his own decision."

"I don't know what is going in his mind but I know he still loves you."

I glanced at Sahil. He was looking towards me. Niya saw me and he dragged Sahil towards me and said, "Ananya I want to dance with my husband now and you can dance with this boring man, who was just staring at you all the time." "I was not staring at her, Niya and I'm not dancing with her." "See Karan I told you, he is a changed man now."

Karan kept one hand on Sahil's shoulder and said, "Sahil what's wrong in dancing with her? She will be gone tomorrow." Sahil looked the other side maybe out of frustration or pain… "Stop fighting both of you," said Niya and pushed me in his arms, "and dance."

"Dance now, you both are dying to be in each other's arms, if not for you both then dance for us please." Niya went to the DJ and said something. Sahil's grip tightened around me looking into my eyes and I moved my hands up and kept them on his shoulders. The lights were dim now, I understood what Niya did. Sahil looked the other side, but I wanted to look him in his eyes and wanted to see love for me one last time, So I placed my hands on his cheeks and made him look into my eyes.

"Look into my eyes, if you are not afraid to acknowledge your feelings."

"I'm not afraid of anything." He was looking into my eyes now. I stepped one foot forward so that I was closer to him. "What are you doing Ananya?" He whispered and I could feel his our breaths soaring high. I was still looking into his eyes and he in mine with so much love. "Kiss me Sahil," I demanded and he shook. I held his hand and dragged him to one corner which was dark enough for nobody to see.

"Kiss me for one last time Sahil, if you ever felt sorry for leaving me." He tightened his grip on my waist and kissed me chastely brushing his lips with mine for a second and then looking into my eyes. My heart was crying now to tell him Sahil I'm so much more in love with you.

I wish you confessed your feeling and stop me from going, I will forgive you for everything, but if you doubt my character, then I will never be yours. Say that you are sorry for what you said Sahil, but he was just staring me into my eyes and I want to just lose myself into his arms as now I was sure he will not say sorry to me and it's the last time I've been in his arms, and thinking this I kissed him. I kissed him the last goodbye kiss, it was a passionate one like our other kisses, but something was lacking in our kiss, maybe due to the pain to leave behind each other ,Sahil was cautious first not responding ,as if he is forcing himself not to kiss me, though he want it badly, but soon he was totally into it, kissing me more passionately as if he also considered it his last kiss with me.

I had reached the moment and it was time for me to take the final decision and I know it was the time to withdraw before it was too late. I broke the kiss with tears in my eyes and pushed Sahil away, who was taken aback by my gesture, but did not do anything to stop me, as he was standing like a statue. The lights got turned on in that moment.

When Ritvik saw me crying, he and Karan ran towards me and Niya towards Sahil who was standing alone on the dance floor.

"Anu, what happened? Is everything all right?" "Nothing Karan I just wanted to go from here and leave all this mess. Our relation is never going to work please don't force me.?" "What is wrong with you Sahil?" shouted Ritvik, "You are a big looser." Karan escorted me outside and Niya came running behind me. "Ananya what happened? What did he say?" "Nothing Niya, he doesn't love me anymore and I just want to leave now."

"No Ananya that's not the truth, please give me some time and I will find out from him.

There must be something that he is hiding. Anu, we both have seen him crying for you. His heart is always yours." "No Niya please don't give me false hope. I want to go home."

"Ok Anu," Said Karan, "Sit in the car," and he gestured Niya to sit with me.

I kept my head on Niya's lap and cried like a baby. It felt like I'm going through the heartbreak again. It was so painful; more than before. I thought that I am completely over Sahil, but I was wrong. I was just bluffing myself. I can't be over him ever, he is a part of my heart now and I can't live without my heart. The place which Sahil had occupied in my heart is like a permanent imprint of his love in my heart. Why do I love him so much after so much have happened in the past few months? Niya was comforting me, but the pain was not stopping, it was worse than the heart attack, the pain of losing someone whom you loved to insanity. Who meant the world to you and suddenly when your world is shattered, you are also completely shattered engulfing in pain. We reached home and Karan dropped me and Niya at the guest house and he went back. I know where he was headed to, but I was now firm with my decision. That man whom I loved so much had no place for me in his heart. "He always does this to me," I said to Niya. "Anu you know how he is. He never tells his problems to anybody. He is alone, handling all the pain. He was the same in college. Remember he loved you so much, but distanced himself from you just because Mrs. Iyer was on the verge of ruining your marks.

But even then he loved you Ananya and now too he loves you, but there may be something which his holding him back."

"No Niya it's over now, I don't want to dwell on Sahil now. You know what hurt me Niya? He doesn't trust me anymore. Being with Sahil will only give me a lot more pain and even if he agrees to marry me, this time my parents will not listen to me and not let me marry him and I don't want to go against my parents, as they had gone through a lot because of me.

I will marry according to them now."

"And do you think Anu you will be happy with that person, when Sahil is still in your heart?" "Who doesn't face heart breaks? I will be fine."

"Anu there is only one man in your life with whom you feel that you are connected with the soul of that person and I know Sahil and you share the same connection."

"Niya please I'm requesting you, close the chapter here and tell me till when are you India?"

"We have come here just for two days, on an official trip by Karan's company. And Ananya mind you if you changed your number and stop talking to me."

"No Niya I would never ever do that again now." I missed my friends dearly.

Niya got a call and she signalled me it was Karan.

"Ok Karan I will be out in 5 min, what did he say? Really!?" said Niya talking to karan and looking at me. "Anu he is coming to take me. You want me to stay back?"

"No Niya its ok, we can meet again tomorrow."

"Ya babes take care I will come tomorrow to meet you."

"Niya what did he say?"

Niya looked at me worried and said, "You really want to know Ananya?" I nodded so she continued, "He said he doesn't want to talk about Ananya anymore."

Niya kissed me on my forehead and hugged me tight and said, "I wish you both were together."

Zoya came after one hour, tired. "Are you ok?" She asked me.

"Yes dear, did you see Sahil?"

"Yes, Sahil sir was looking quite upset when Karan sir was talking to him but he pushed him and went outside."

Ohh gosh Sahil what did you do? That's why Karan was sounding a bit angry and that's why Niya left. She continued, "Ritvik shouted at Sahil before going that you are going to regret it for your whole life bhai hurting a girl like her twice. You have gone out of your mind and he too left in anger with his girlfriend."

Oh gosh, tears sprawled down from my cheeks. My Sahil is alone now, everybody walked out of his life, he will be so lonely again.

"Ananya ma'am," said Zoya and she hugged me and we both cried.

I for losing my Sahil and she for seeing me break like this.

Chapter 25

We all got ready in the morning and keeping our luggage in the bus we all got collected in the main hall. Everybody was there except my Sahil.

Samar congratulated us for our hard work and success and thanked us for our strong determination, but my eyes were just glued on the staircase just to get one last glimpse of him. Samar was shaking hands one by one with each employee. Ridhima was after him.

When Samar stood in front of me, I could see my Sahil's elder brother and not my sir.

He shook his hand and told me, "He will not come Ananya." He had noticed me looking towards the stairs. I got so weak that I hugged Samar tightly and started sobbing.

Seeing this Ridhima signalled the others to leave and she started patting my back. Samar also got emotional with me and I could see tears clouding his eyes.

"I don't understand why Sahil is letting you go," said Samar wiping my tears. "You want to meet him, he is in his room," Said Ridhima.

"No, ma'am please I can't handle his rudeness anymore," and bidding them adieu, I came out of the house crying and climbed on the bus.

Kavya commented, "My God! This woman is something, all man, are mad for him." "Except Sahil," Added Natasha.

"What did she think? If I did not get Sahil she will get him?" Said Natasha.

This time Manoj asked Natasha to be quite.

We all boarded the plane and here I was heartbroken and far away from my Sahil forever, praying to God that I shouldn't ever meet him again in this life, but my love will always be pure for him and nobody can take that place ever in my heart again. With this deep pain in my heart I reached Delhi.

I called mom once I reached Delhi.

Richa had informed me that she had left the flat as her parents wants her to stay with them before going to Austria. I was alone in my flat now, still thinking about Sahil that he did not come to see me, how can he be so hard hearted. After crying and thinking a lot I decided I will not let Sahil's thoughts ruin my life again and here I was with my same old life .

My office, my cabin…I don't need to share it with arrogant Sahil.

Everybody gave me a different look now as Kavya and Natasha had told nonsense, but I didn't care, not anymore.

There was a meeting in the morning with our Chairman who congratulated us on our hard work and success and wish us to carry on the same hard work.

Zoya came to my cabin along with Vikram and wished me.

"Zoya don't you dare call me ma'am again."

"Ok Ananya," Vikram was shocked.

"I'm not so bad Vikram," I said and in return he gave me his embarrassed smile.

Manoj called me in his cabin and gave me a worrried look.

"Ananya, I had approved your leave for one week."

"Manoj, I'm not going anywhere."

"But I thought you needed a break."

"I needed it at that time, but not now, when I'm no more with that moron."

"Who Sahil?" He said at once and regretted.

"I'm sorry Ananya for being personal but you need a break."

"You want me to go into depression? If I will continue working, I will forget everything."

He studied me for a minute and then nodded.

I burdened myself with work to forget my Sahil.

I was again on the verge of being antisocial, but I just didn't feel like interacting much with anybody. Ritvik was sent to our Noida branch to handle the pressure of the employees.

Natasha and Kavya were as mean as ever, but it really didn't matter now.

I was sitting and brooding about my past when my phone rang and brought me back to reality.

"Ananya there is a meeting as few new people are joining our team and there is this new guy in a finance team, which you need to assist and help him and explain about the work you do."

"Are you firing me Manoj?" I said, worried.

"Ananya you are so funny? I can't even dream to fire you. There was a lot of work load on you so I requested the seniors to scuffle your work load and some new assignments are yet to arrive and you need a large team to handle it. New trainees are also hired."

No! Now I would need to share my cabin I don't know with whom. Then I remembered how I used to make Sahil irritate in his cabin.

Natasha and Kavya were gossiping as usual.

"Hey, I heard the man who is coming in the finance team is super hot."

"Wow, really but he will be sitting with Ananya and you know how she is mad about hot men."

"Mind your language Kavya."

"Omg I'm so sorry, Ananya see no man is interested in you. You are so damn boring."

"Really? And what about you Kavya?" I retaliated in my sharp voice.

"Guys, please stop this nonsense here." Shouted Manoj seeing our vice president.

"So we all our gathered here to welcome some new people in our team, who are highly efficient and experienced and give their valuable services and help us in undertaking new financial assignments." A tall man came inside who was in his mid thirties with a beard and pony. "He is Mr. Ramcharan and Natasha he will be working along with you for hiring and looking after the employee grievances."

Natasha gave him a not so inviting smile.

Good enjoy his company I mouthed it to Natasha and she made a face and looked the other way, and one by one all the trainees and the other staff was introduced.

I was waiting for my partner. "Some of you must know him," said our vice president introducing the finance person, I could see a look of horror on Kavya and Natasha's a face and Manoj was looking towards me and smiling. What was wrong with them and I looked back and froze. "Here is Mr. Sahil who was in Bangalore with you all he will be joining the finance team." Zoya stood up and screeched a yeah making the CEO look towards her with wide eyes.

Sahil gave Zoya a shake of his hand and I saw Vikram pulling her down on her seat.

Sahil raised his eyebrows looking towards me. I was still in shock.

"Miss Ananya," called the president but I was in a comatose.

"Miss Ananya…" he said a little louder and brought me back. "Yes sir."

"Mr. Sahil will work along with you in your finance team and he will share the cabin with you as you both have already worked together. I hope there is no problem."

And before I could say anything my Sahil spoke "No sir, there is no problem between us. In fact we share a very good rapport working together, right Ananya?" He smiled.

I smiled back and nodded.

Natasha came to greet Sahil but my stubborn Sahil moved away from her and she stormed out of the conference room.

Manoj came towards me smiling, and I said you were knowing right.

"Manoj can you please show me the way to Miss Ananya's cabin."

"Sorry Sahil I can't help you with this."

"Ananya is the right person to show you the cabin," and he left.

Seeing Sahil, Zoya came running towards us and said, "Hi Sahil sir, I'm so happy to see you here," And she hugged him slightly.

Sahil was happy and he patted her back.

Zoya looked at me mouthed a sorry.

"How are you Zoya and how do you work with people who wear Mickey mouse night suit at night?"

"Mr. Sahil you are crossing all your limits. Don't forget that there was a Mickey mouse on your cake as well."

"It was for you baby," and they both laughed. "Grow up miss Ananya and please lead me the way to our cabin."

"Excuse me not ours, it's mine."

"Ya, whatever," He said

"Come," I said and took him to my cabin.

"You got such a small cabin Ananya."

"This is not Bangalore, sir and this is Delhi the overcrowded city and now tell me what brought you here."

"My work brought me here Ananya and nothing else; please don't keep any doubt in your mind that I came because of you."

"That is least expected of you Mr. Sahil, who did not come to say bye."

"Oh miss Ananya, I don't do childish things."

"I got a better opportunity here so I joined and my relatives are also living here, I hope you remember."

"Let me explain about the work."

"Can you please bring a coffee for me Ananya?"

"Hello!? Company has not hired me as your secretary. Go and get it yourself from the right corner."

"Miss Ananya, don't be so rude. Remember I brought coffee for you once."

"Ok, fine I'm going, but this will be the last time."

I brought two cups of coffee and when I came in my table was so clean, all my files were neatly placed over one another and my pens and other stuff were kept neatly.

I did not know that my table got so much space, but it infuriated me.

"What the hell Sahil, how dare you mess up with my table?"

"How could you work with so much clutter on the desk?"

"Oh please Mr. Sahil this is my cabin I don't need your OCD skills here."

"Miss Ananya, now I will be working with you and I need the table clean."

"Oh God, Sahil have you come here to irritate me?"

"Wow! Instead of thanking me for cleaning your desk you are shouting at me. Thank God I did not marry you otherwise I would have had to clean the rooms all the day."

It was enough now. I picked up a file and threw it at him. But cleverly he bent down and the file went on Manoj's face. "Oh God! Shit!" I shouted.

Manoj gave me a cold stare and then said, "Ananya lower down your volume. You can be heard shouting outside."

"I'm sorry Manoj, but please I can't work with him. See what he did with my desk."

"Wow, Ananya for the first time I'm seeing your desk so clean and I think you should thank Sahil for this."

"Manoj he has come here to irritate me."

" Ananya you have no choice."

After explaining him the work we both started reading our files, then suddenly he asked me where was I staying here.

I raised my eyebrow and told him its none of his business.

"Ok, actually I don't have a place in Delhi right now and my relatives stay quite far, so I was thinking if you could allow me to stay at your place for one day?" He asked.

"Unbelievable, how can you even ask me that? Shameless man."

"I'm not taking you to my house at all, and you are paid enough that you can stay at a hotel for one night."

"Please, I will not tell anybody. My brother also let you live in our house."

"I can't believe this Sahil! You have no shame."

"Ananya have you forgotten that you stayed in my room for one night when there was no key to your room?"

"Why can't you go to a hotel?"

"I don't want to eat boring food there. I want to cook myself and eat and you won't have to cook."

He remembered I didn't like to cook.

I was amazed by his behaviour, but I said yes because I knew he will eat my brains out until I say yes. I know if he wants something he will continue pestering me like this. And secondly, he promised he will cook dinner and breakfast, as I knew he cooks really well, and even I wanted to eat food cooked by him.

At 7 I stood up and said let's go.

He obeyed me dutifully and asked innocently, "How do you go to the bus stop?"

"I have a car. I earn enough to buy a car."

"Ohh thank god," He said. "I thought I would have to go in a bus."

I was about to sit in the driving seat, he came forward and said, "Let me drive. I don't want to die."

"Mr. Sahil this is my car and if you want to stay at my house, you will have to sit in my car quietly."

He grinned and said, "I can do anything to spend one night with you.

"I mean in your house." He was quick to amend.

He was quiet on the way and kept looking out of the window.

"Wow, Delhi has changed a lot, but the traffic is still the same."

I parked my car in front of my flat.

"How do you manage to stay here alone?" He asked.

"I was staying with a roomy but now she is getting married so she has left."

"Ohh, and when are you getting married?"

"Sahil do you want to spend the whole night outside?"

"No," he said squeezing his nose and quietly went along with me inside.

He was shocked to see the condition of my room when I switched on the light.

The bedding was half lying on the bed and half on the floor.

My make up things were sprawled on the table and my cupboard was opened with clothes falling out.

"Ananya, you have some kind of disorder," He said quietly.

"Sahil please stop commenting and that is your bed," I pointed towards Richa's bed.

He gave me a disappointed look and said I can't sleep on this dirty bed.

"Look Sahil this is what I can give you if you want to take it its ok."

He gave me his wickedest grin and said, "You can give me a lot Ananya."

"Are you flirting with me?"

"I dare not do that. You don't mind sleeping with me in the same room?"

"We are sleeping in the same room but on different beds and I'm just letting you sleep here for one night as you also let me sleep once with you."

He made a small face and said, "We have slept together many times. If you don't mind, we can even share the bed as the bed sheet of your bed is cleaner than this one."

"How dare you?" I threw a pillow on his face. "Either sleep on that bed, or get out of here."

"Ok, fine. I will sleep here."

"What about dinner?" he quipped.

"What about dinner? You said you are going to prepare it."

"Ya right, but what do you want to eat?"

"You can make maggi, if you are tired."

"What!" He was shocked. "Do you eat such unhealthy things during night? That's why you have gained so much weight."

"Ohh hello! I'm not fat. I was reducing your work."

"Ananya will you not cook after marriage as well?"

I gave him a look and he just turned the question around, "I mean with the person you will get married to."

"Women like me are rare to find, that's why I'm still single Sahil."

"I would have considered of marrying you Ananya but looking at your life style I can't marry you."

I threw a pillow at him and said "I'm not going to marry you Mr. arrogant."

He went into the kitchen and was a little disgusted not to find any vegetables in the fridge.

"Ananya I can't cook things which are not present."

I did not get time to buy vegetables yesterday, but he was relieved to find eggs in my fridge and so he took out three eggs broke them into the bowl mixed them and quickly made two yummy omelettes for us.

"So how is it?" he asked me after finishing the omelette.

Sahil again seemed to be a changed person, he was behaving just like my old Sahil, who cared and love me so much.

Did he had a change of mind, is this the reason he is here. "Ananya I just asked you how is the omelette , you can think about my behaviour later on."

How come this nerd reads my mind?

"I was not thinking about you and the omelette is so good."

"Thank you."

"Now I'm so tired I'm going to sleep." "Ohh God, Ananya don't you brush at night?"

"I brush only in the morning." "Anu how could you be so careless with your health?"

"Sahil please I'm not your girlfriend, so stop lecturing me." "If you were my girlfriend would you have obeyed me?" "I would have done anything for you Sahil," and we got serious looking towards each there. "Ya I know that," and then he changed the topic, "Do you have an extra clean bed sheet that I can put on this dirty bed? We were interrupted by my mother's call.

I gestured to Sahil to be quiet. "Hi mom, How are you?"

"I'm fine beta. Anu can you come to Jaipur for two days?"

"What are you saying mom? I can't come, I am too busy but why are you asking me to come are you both ok?"

"Ya beta don't worry we are ok."

"Ananya you promised me that you will get married after returning from Bangalore with a guy of my choice." "Mom please don't irritate me, I'm tired." "Anu listen," She was cold now, "Day after tomorrow a boy is coming to meet you. We had already met him and he is a nice guy. He saw your pic and he also liked you. His family is coming and we have fixed your marriage."

"What mumma!? How can you do this with me? How can I marry a man without even meeting him?" Sahil gave me his arched look. "Mumma, please I'm not going to stay in Jaipur after marriage." "He stays in Delhi Ananya." "Ok, so let me meet him in Delhi first."

"Ananya if you have a little respect for your mother you will come and do what I say."

"I want to get you married next month," and she hung up.

"Ananya, are you ok?": Asked Sahil seeing me like a statue.

"How can she fix my marriage without letting me meet the boy!

"I'm getting married Sahil, to a man I don't even know."

Sahil stood up from the bed and looked at me and said, "You should have been married by now Ananya. Your mother must have searched a good boy for you."

I switched off the light in disgust, without listening to him further.

"Ananya, where is your Mickey mouse night suit?"

"Shut up and let me sleep."

Chapter 26

I woke up in the morning and saw that Sahil was ready.

"Get up, sleepy head. You will be late."

Wow, it was a fine sight; I wish I could get up every day looking at him.

"Ananya its 8.30; w

e need to go to the office."

"Ohh, why you did not wake me up?"

"Who wakes you up every day?"

I quickly got up and took 15 min to get ready.

"You need breakfast," He stood up and brought a plate of cheese sandwich.

"Bravo Sahil! You made breakfast for me!"

I took the sandwich in the car and allowed Sahil to drive my car.

"So, you will apply for leave today?"

I had no choice, now I had left everything in my mother's hand.

Anu if you want, we can marry right now.

I choked on my sandwich. "Amazing! I was mistreated by you in Bangalore, you thought I had an affair with Ritvik and now you come to Delhi and ask me to marry you! And do you think I will say yes to you?"

"Of course Anu because I know you love me and I love you."

Whoa Sahil you realized this so soon.

"It's not too late Ananya, at least I'm saying it out to you."

"Sahil you behaved so badly with me in Bangalore."

"Ya, I know Anu and I'm so sorry for it. When I kissed you on my birthday, did you not feel my love towards you?"

"I did Sahil but your reactions were so confusing. You did not even come to say good bye."

"That's because it was difficult for me to see you go again from my life."

"But anyway, I think you are right, we love each other and will always do that, but I think we can't live together."

I looked at him questioningly.

"I mean the way you live so untidily." He laughed.

"Ohh, just shut up."

"Seriously Ananya, do something before your marriage, otherwise what will happen to that guy whom you are about to marry?"

"Don't worry Sahil I will teach him to do household chores like you."

I felt bad that Sahil could have tried better to convince me to marry him, but I guess he was not so interested and he is right. We both fight all the time.

"Sahil if you want, you can stay in my flat while I'm in Jaipur?"

"Thanks Anu, but I have found a flat in the same locality."

"That was quick."

"Ohh Manoj help me out for this."

I applied for 1 week leave and it was easily approved as I took little leaves.

It was strange but my mood had completely uplifted by Sahil's presence.

Oh god, why had he come here? Now I had to see him every day after my marriage, how would I forget him? I should start searching for new jobs.

I came to my cabin with a coffee, Sahil was busy with the new trainee explaining them their job profile.

I sat on the last chair and stared at my cute Sahil, while sipping my coffee.

He saw me staring but he ignored. He was finished giving his presentation and when the trainee left, he asked, "Why were you staring Miss Ananya?"

I said nothing.

"So, you got the leave?"

"Yes, I'm going tomorrow morning."

"All the best for your new life."

"When will you marry, Sahil?"

"After you Anu. Samar is also searching for a girl for me and I know he is gonna choose a nice one."

I felt like somebody pushed me into the chilled water, and I stood up and hugged Sahil tightly.

"I will miss you always Sahil," He hugged me back and said, "I will miss you too Ananya, but it is better that we don't marry each other."

Manoj came inside and that was our oops moment.

Sahil at once left me and I straightened my hair.

Ananya I came to say bye to you said Manoj embarrassed.

Thanks Manoj and he soon left us alone."Happy journey Anu," said Sahil and I took my bag with pain in my heart and tears in my eyes.

I know I would be resigning as soon as I leave this premises.

I won't be able to see Sahil again. I was not able to sleep the whole night, with heavy heart I reached the bus stop and climbed the bus and sat in the last window seat, the pain was getting difficult to bear now. Tears were not stopping. Ohh, Sahil I love you and want to marry you, why were you so reluctant to marry me. I would have definitely said yes, if you had pressurized me and looked into my eyes and asked me to marry you. I knew he loved me, but why was he not ready to marry me then?

The whole journey went thinking about Sahil and I reached my home town.

I saw papa standing at the bus stop and he gave me a meek smile when he saw me.

I ran and hugged him tightly. "Papa, I missed you so much." "Me too. Why are your eyes red?" I smiled and ignored the question.

I reached home and maa was sitting in the living room, she came and hugged me and told me how much she had missed me.

Aryan came running towards me and picked me in his strong arms, he has been going to the gym a lot and looked handsome. He was working with an MNC in Pune.

"Hey di! How are you doing? All good na?" My little grown up brother asked.

"Yes, I'm all good. So, did you tell mom about your girlfriend?"

He smiled coyly and said, "Yes, di she will be coming in your marriage."

I held his hand and said, "Aryan don't ever break her heart." There were tears in my eyes.

Aryan wiped my tears and said, "Di now no more crying. You will get everything now. Just let go the past di," With tears in his eyes he hugged me.

I remember how my little brother cried seeing me break down for Sahil, he was furious at Sahil. But he is right now it was time to let go everything and I don't want to snatch away the happiness from them just because I was not happy.

"You have worked very hard Ananya now it's time to move on."

"Ya, maa right, I will marry the boy whom you have chosen."

"Thank you, Ananya you made me so happy today, but what happened you seem so distracted and lost? What's going on inside of you? I'm your mother beta, please share with me."

"No, maa there is nothing."

"Anu if you do not like the boy you can say no, I will not force you, beta."

"No, maa its ok I'm, ok whoever you chose for me."

Next day was quiet a hectic one; as maa was busy decorating the house with flowers. "Maa why are you doing all this? Please keep it simple."

"Beta it is your roka, please be cheerful now, and Anu did you bring that pink saree which I told to bring."

"Maa please, I'm not wearing that saree for God's sake. You know who gave it to me."

"Ya, I know. Well just forget about him. He is gone long away, do you still remember him?"

"No mom, not exactly."

"So that's it, beta. You are wearing this one. You look so beautiful in it." I got ready wearing that saree and for a fleeting moment, I remembered what Sahil said when he gave me the saree – 'You will look like a princess wearing this. I had asked, When will I wear it? And he had said, you can wear it on our roka baby and that had made me cry,' and today also I cried missing my Sahil. I had not imagined that I will wear this saree for somebody else. Somehow, I managed to control myself and got ready.

Maa was running here and there preparing for the visit. She halted seeing me and came close and hugged me. "Ananya, you are looking so beautiful, just that your smile is missing. But don't worry, when you will meet the boy your smile will come back. He is very good looking." "Ohh come on maa, stop it." Though I was ready on the outside, but inside I was in pain, every single nerve in my heart was bleeding and was ready to burst, making me lose my ground, was this love pain and it was worse than a heart attack. I felt like crying, why is love so painful, I wish I could stop this feeling of being in love and I felt so broken from within, as the pain was so excruciating, making my every single nerve crack with ache. The door bell rang and, In a few minutes I could hear soft voices. We had not called any other guest only my father's sister Roma bua was there. Roma bua came in and said, "Ananya, you are so lucky, he is very handsome."

"Come, let's go out." How stupid I was, I had not even asked what does he do.

"How many people are there Roma bua?"

"Beta don't get nervous."

"No, I'm asking just like this. His brother and bhabhi and his friend and his wife have come."

"Ohh, what about his parents? Anu I don't know. They are not there, he doesn't have his father and I don't know about his mother. Bhaiya said not to ask him about his mother."

If Sahil would have come to see me, he would have also not have brought his mother.

I am still remembering that jerk, on my roka, Anu get a grip! "Chale?" asked Roma Bua.

"Keep your eyes down while walking." "What bua, come on."

I was led into the room full of people, but now I was damn nervous and could not raise my eyes and look up. All my confidence which I used to have in, the board rooms was all gone.

"Come Ananya," said my mother and she made me sit on the sofa along with the boy and I was still not able to raise my head and look at him. All I could see was his sharp black pointed shoes. I don't even feel like looking at his face. "Ananya, at least see your future husband," my bua teased me and everybody started laughing.

"One lady came and stood in front of me and she was holding a beautiful pink colour duppatta in her hands. I had never imagined myself that I will be so nervous. Crap Sahil I wish you had come here for the roka, I would have been sitting here confidently I closed my eyes when the lady wearing a pink colour suit draped me with the pink dupatta. "Ananya, you are looking beautiful." Her voice seems so familiar to me. I opened my eyes, which had tears flowing as I lost my breath seeing Ridhima in front of me. She smiled seeing me like a statue and kissed me on my forehead.

I looked at the boy and there was my stupid Sahil sitting there and grinning and then I saw Samar bhaiya, Karan and Niya. I didn't know what to do, I was so shocked that I covered my face with my hands and started crying. "Ohh Anu stop it," said Sahil and he came closer and brought his hands encircling me. I removed my hands from my face and buried my face in his chest and hugged him tightly crying like a baby. He kissed me on my forehead and said, "Hey you will spoil your make up." I was in no mood to let him go as I held him so tightly as if he was about to run. Niya came near me and said, "Anu your parents are watching," And I composed myself, wiping my tears. My mother was having tears in her eyes, "Anu did you like the boy? You have time you can think about it." "No mom," I said instantly and everybody started laughing. My little brother came and hugged me and said, "Di, see I told you, it's time to be happy now." I pulled his ear and said, "You all knew it." After the roka ceremony we went out together for lunch leaving my parents behind. We all sat in the car. Everybody was laughing at me. "I hate you guys. You all knew it and nobody informed me and Sahil you jerk, you stayed with me at my house and was pretending to be so innocent." "Anu, how could you think that I will let you go so this time again?"

"Tell me all please, this is so confusing." I was eager to know.

"I'll tell you," said Niya. "After you returned to Delhi, Karan, Samar, Ridhima, Ritvik and I went to Sahil's room and started questioning him for his behaviour. We even took the help of Reem who forced Sahil to speak out. He then told us that Ananya's mother called him as somebody told her that you both were having an affair. Your mother pleaded with Sahil to stay away from you. Aunty made him promise that he will make you feel that he is not interested in you at all. And this was the reason Mr Sahil was avoiding you and suffering day by day."

"And a special thanks to Ritvik," said Samar. "What about him?" I asked.

"He was the one who convinced Sahil by telling him that you are still in love with Sahil and you would have said yes to Sahil had he tried to ask her and he also said to Sahil that is your love so weak that you cannot go and convince her parents. Make them trust you; make them realize that it's only you who could make their daughter happy. Don't sit like a loser here crying and brooding for your whole life. If not for you, think about the poor girl who still loves you and whom you deserted once leaving her in so much pain, but her love for you is still the same. Don't ruin her life once again and force her to marry anybody else.

She will not be happy and you also know that." That was the time Ananya said, I thought that Ritvik was right and I was so wrong thinking badly about you both." "So, that same day I packed my bag and came here to Jaipur. Uncle and aunty were angry with me, but I told them, how I was forced to marry and I genuinely love your daughter and she also loves me and it will be of no use if you marry her with somebody else and she will not be happy with that guy. They said they need to ask you." "So, what did you say?" "I said that she will say yes, I know her, she still loves me." "And then you came to Delhi you jerk."

"There was an opening in your branch I applied for the transfer and luckily I got it."

"You are so mean Sahil." He embraced me, encircling me in his arms and said, "Oh baby, I love you so much."

"Sahil have you forgotten all your respect for your elders? And there was a smile on everybody's face. "So you both can get married after six months," Said Samar.

"What!?" Shrieked Sahil, "No ways."

"Is it too early Sahil? You need more time?" Asked Niya teasing my Sahil.

"Please Niya, 6 months is a long time. I'm getting married next month."

"Sahil, you are so eager to marry her!" Said Ridhima, smiling.

"Bhabhi, I have already waited too long for her," And everybody started laughing.

I requested Sahil to call his mother as well on our marriage as my wedding present and

somehow, after coaxing, he managed to say yes.

We both got married in Jaipur with our close relative, as neither Sahil nor I wanted to get married on a big scale.

It was Sunday morning and I felt somebody was shaking me.

I opened one eye and saw my Sahil with a cup of coffee in his hands, "Ananya please wake up. What's the time Sahil?"

"It's 6 in the morning, we need to go for a jog you promised me."

"Not today Sahil, please let me sleep and I covered my face with the pillow."

He removed my pillow and he kissed me on my lips.

"Wake up lazy bones, you have been promising me for the past one month, since we got married, that you will go on a morning jog with me."

"Oh Sahil, I regret marrying you now," and I opened my arms and said please come to me.

He kept his coffee and layed on the bed and cuddled me in his embrace.

His arms were the best place for me. I kissed him on his cheeks and said making love to you is better than jogging. He looked into my eyes and said, "You naughty girl, you are spoiling me as well." "Yes, my love," and we kissed like never before.

"I love you Sahil."

"I love you too Ananya."

About the Author

Nidhi was born in Jhansi and her schooling was done from Saint Francis Convent School. She now resides in Gurgaon along with her family. Few short stories written by her have already been published and this is her first independent novel - Born To Be Yours.